THE
TREASURE-TROVE
TALES

At the Gazebo

Katelyn Emily

First published by Dog Ear Publishing
4010 W. 86th Street, Ste H
Indianapolis, IN 46268
www.dogearpublishing.net

ISBN: 978-159858-940-5

This book is printed on acid-free paper.

The characters and events portrayed in this book are fictitious. Any simi-larity to real persons, living or dead is coincidental and not intended by the author.

Printed in the United States of America

Send any author e-mail correspondence to CORELTD@PTD.NET

To all young, aspiring authors who decided that adulthood was just a bit too far off to wait.

Also, to my past English teachers. You have inspired me more than you will ever know and I will be forever grateful.

To my biggest fan
and fellow Disney-
lover!!! Sorry it took
four months for me
to finally do this
(I was hoping you'd
forget)

♡ Katie
Emily
Sheinberg

Acknowledgments

I would like to especially thank my mother,
who believed in my book and helped bring it to life.
If it wasn't for you, this story would still be on my computer,
instead of on a shelf.

Also, many thanks to all my friends and family
who kindly took the time to read through my very first,
and rather rough, draft. Your feedback was much appreciated.

Part 1

The Discovery

Prologue

It's funny how something seemingly simple and ordinary has, in fact, the ability to change a person's perspective on life. For instance, a well-known car salesman might one day notice an open book of Shakespeare in a shop window on his way to work and suddenly realize that his true passion lies with the stage. Or perhaps, a mother of three might glance at one of her children's pretend campaign posters and decide suddenly that she should embark upon a political career, such as running for mayor.

Our seemingly meaningless object however is not a book of plays, nor is it an advertisement. Others might glance at our item, shake their heads, and wonder to themselves why such smart kids were wasting their time with such a curious hobby. To my siblings and me, however, our object meant so much more.

I used to sometimes ponder the phrase 'Don't judge a book by its cover.' While at times this statement is unquestionably true, I couldn't help but realize that this is not always the case. Isn't it true, after all, that a person arriving at a 'black tuxedo preferred' party in sweatpants and a t-shirt can most likely be dubbed 'careless,' at least when it comes to proper dress codes? Or what about the essay assignment that was handed in, written in crayon on a crumpled up napkin? Wouldn't it be correct of the teacher to assume that the work was done hastily on the bus that morning?

My older brother often teases me for thinking too much. Sometimes I think he may be right.

In any case, I am certain that when it comes to my family and the object that we so treasure, the phrase 'Don't judge a book by its cover' is 100 percent accurate.

I always pictured my first book being a mystery novel: some elaborate, heart-pounding story set in a luxurious hotel, on a romantic cruise, or in an ancient castle. Something along the lines of Agatha Christie. I suppose I can blame my mother for this ambition, for it was she who too loved mysteries and soon transferred her passion to me. At night, when she came in to tuck me in, we would often stay awake into the night reading a thrilling story.

But sometimes, when a story is laid out before your eyes, it is a crime not to write it down, despite its genre.

Memories. I can still feel my mother's soft touch as she stroked my hair until I fell asleep on nights when I woke up from a scary dream. I can still smell my father's cologne that was so pungent when he lifted me up and swung me around and around. Often, I am overcome by such a strong remembrance of my parents that I feel dizzy and have to sit down.

Memories. They are both a gift and a curse. The former so as not to forget the ones we love and the latter because often they seem to make the pain of loss too much to bear. But that is why we have each other, and for this, I am thankful.

My sister Amanda, though everyone calls her Mandy, is the oldest of the Avery clan. I do not believe she has a shy bone in her body and often I am envious of her bravado. She is intelligent, loving, and has always truly realized the importance of us sticking together, even when the rest of us were blinded. At thirteen years old, she already acts like an adult, and has become something of a mother figure to us. When she does get bossy, though, my brother Sean never has a problem straightening her out.

A year younger than Amanda, Sean has always been the adventurer of the family. When we were younger, he used to run around the house, 'saving' everyone from danger. Though this would more often provoke annoyance rather than appreciation, it proved early on that he had a caring heart. Rarely showing fear, Sean is the shoulder which we lean against. His mirthful and amusing attitude toward life now and then makes me slightly jealous of him as well, which afterward makes me question my own self-confidence at this sibling envy.

Danielle at nine has often been labeled the 'odd one' out of our sibling pact because of her different appearance from the rest of us. Unlike our dark, chocolate-colored, straight hair and brown eyes, her hair is a very light brown with thick, curly locks and her eyes are hazel. I could tell very early on that Danielle did not like to be singled out as the *different* one, but it took others much longer to realize that their statements, which were meant to be taken frivolously, were in fact doing much damage. Once she got to a certain age, Danielle would not look us in the eye, and hardly spoke when she was in our company. I have heard from others that at school she has a good sense of humor and makes friends easily, but for a while, I saw none of this. Instead, my younger sister became especially close to our parents, who also sensed that she was hurting, and showered her with affection.

Next, there is TJ. A little ball of fun, Timothy Jacob is four years old. He always seems to have a place inside him where backup, nonstop energy is stored. As the baby of the family, he has only known what it is like to have people coo and fuss over him. He seems to most certainly not mind it. And what four-year-old wouldn't love having multiple siblings that are always around to be his never-ending playmates? We often take turns watching over him. It was long ago that we realized TJ has more liveliness than all of us combined. Multiplied by ten. Plus two cups of coffee. We also learned that it is quite impossible to stay mad at him, especially if he comes to you, lifts his small arms upwards, and wraps them tightly around your neck when you pick him up. No one can compete with the apologetic hug of tiny TJ.

And lastly, there is me. Julia Anne Avery. The 'gentle, compassionate, quiet one.' This is what I have been categorized as by everyone for so long, that I've come to describe myself in that way as well. With the same medium-length, dark brown hair as Mandy, and the same features (though I tend to think of mine as a bit more relaxed), I have often been thought of as a smaller, calmer replica of her. At eleven, I have never felt the resentfulness toward my siblings that I've heard of other middle children experiencing. In fact, I've always found it to be rather silly. Being the middle child is great; it's smack-dab in the middle of being treated like a baby and having the responsibilities of the older kids. Although I appear quiet and reserved on the outside, I have numerous opinions and thoughts of my own within. In truth, it is just that I feel more comfortable opening up to my family and close friends, than to every single stranger in public that I meet. I enjoy reading, especially mystery novels (as previously noted), eating chocolate by the boxful, and painting. Spiders are a no, along with anything that has six or more legs, and so are extreme heights, though I can deal with the occasional small roller coaster without screaming too much, when forced to by Sean.

I used to wonder if people truly changed after a traumatic event, if they became different people, with different thoughts and different interests. I never imagined, however, that I'd experience it first-hand. The truth is, everyone handles things differently, and one of the hardest things in the world may just be trying to rise up again after you have fallen.

After our parents died, in many ways we did change. It felt like a part of us had died along with them, and for a time, we were not quite sure what was expected of us as life went on. I could hardly believe that the supermarket was still open, that the laundry still needed to be done, that school would start in the fall, that the sun still rose and set, and that the Earth continued to turn...

Life went on for everyone else as usual. But not for us. And it took something seemingly meaningless to help us through our time of need.

So here is our story. We were the Avery children: alone, confused, and in possession of a single, transparent jar filled to the brim with multi-colored pebbles, and an unusual assortment of strange trinkets that would soon, to us, mean the world.

Chapter 1

June

I woke up with eyes red from crying, as I had every night for the past two weeks. I had trouble recalling where I was at first, but relaxed under my temporary shield of unawareness, lowering my eyelids slowly.

I had always found the lack of clarity that I often had the privilege of experiencing when I woke up both strange and disturbing. Sometimes, I would randomly awaken in the middle of the night, and in an utterly confused state, begin to get dressed for school, wondering why on earth my alarm hadn't gone off.

Though usually I would perform my customary routine of blinking hard, shaking my head, and waiting impatiently for my memory to return, today I welcomed my ignorance.

My eyelids fluttered softly and my gaze slowly drifted toward the walls surrounding my bed. It was then that I saw the colored pencil sketches and macaroni art in bronze picture frames, mementos from my father's childhood. At that moment, I remembered that I was at our grandparents' house, and the shield was broken.

It was hard to believe that it had only been two weeks since our parents died, instead of an eternity or two. Just two weeks since we received the telephone call from the police department.

Though I tried to forget, I could see the scene replay time and again in my mind. I wondered if it would ever let me be.

We had been sleeping over at our grandparents' house the night of the accident. Mandy, Sean, Danielle, TJ, and me. Grandma and Grandpa lived about five blocks away from our house.

I remembered that it was stormy, but I had always liked the rain. I loved the sound it made on my window as I fell asleep; it made me feel secure and comforted in my room. And rain meant that we wouldn't need to water the plants in our front yard the next day. One less chore to do, the better.

The weather hadn't started off that badly, but it had become increasingly windy and wet as the night wore on. It ended up being one of the stormiest nights Springfield, Pennsylvania had seen in a long time.

I remembered holding my little brother close and feeling his small body trembling against mine as each bright bolt of lightening lit up the sky and booms of thunder rocked the house. Snug under our covers, we were safe and felt content. We had no possible way of knowing, no slight reason to expect, that a huge, lightning-struck tree in our backyard would fall onto our house. It would collapse the roof, set the house on fire, burning our lives, dreams, and memories to the ground.

I slowly shook my head from side to side, trying and failing to release the picture from my mind.

I got out of my father's old bed and began getting dressed quietly, so as not to wake the sleeping Mandy on the aged couch in the corner. My clothing choices were beyond limited. We each had only a pair of nighttime attire, and an extra set for the daytime; the same clothes we had been wearing the day of the storm. Our grandparents had not yet had time to take us shopping due to the commotion and disorder of the past two weeks. Usually Mandy, who detested extreme disorder, would be going crazy at all the disarray, but she seemed to barely notice.

After brushing my teeth with a spare toothbrush and borrowing my grandmother's ancient brush, its bristles twisted and bent, I made my way to the kitchen in search of breakfast. As I walked along unhurriedly, a wave of nausea swept over me at the thought of what the rest of my life would be like without parents.

I shook my head to clear my thoughts and picked up my pace, eyes open, but not quite looking ahead. As a result, I almost bumped into my grandfather, who also was making his way down the hall. He smiled sadly at me and touched my arm before rushing on, as if he too were running away from his thoughts.

I knew how difficult this was for my grandparents. Losing a son and a daughter-in-law and being suddenly responsible for five children must have been more than overwhelming. Somehow, though, they managed to put on a strong face and show little of the despair they must have been going through.

I came up to the pantry and checked to see what was edible. No cereal. No pop tarts. No granola bars. Only a can of tomato sauce, two boxes of spaghetti, a container of spiced peaches, and an unopened bottle of soda. I scurried to the refrigerator and was displeased to find that its contents were even less promising than the cabinet. I decided that the spiced peaches would suffice and grabbed the jar, which was the thick, old-fashioned type.

The piles of food that the neighbors had brought over was almost entirely finished and I made a mental note to remind my grandparents to go food shopping, even before we worried about getting new clothing. 'TJ the picky eater,' a nickname that was bestowed upon him for reasons that do not need to be explained, would most certainly not enjoy the current grocery selection.

Retrieving a spoon from the utensil drawer, I sat down at the table, closed my eyes, and saw nothing, just blackness.

Nothing. Absolutely nothing. Those words were haunting.

I could feel distressing thoughts creeping back into my conscience and I knew that this time, nodding them off would not work. I told myself that we still had each other, but my heart refused to listen. The complete bleakness of the truth of our situation dawned on me like the dark gloom of a storm descending over a bright blue sky.

Nothing. We had nothing of ours left. The only house that we had ever known was gone, as were all of our toys and games, artwork, old report cards, posters, sports ribbons, piano. Every small, trivial thing that would now mean a great deal to us if we could just hold them again was gone forever.

And of course, we had no parents.

How could a whole lifetime be erased in just one night?

Then a new thought came to me so suddenly that I felt a throbbing pain. I instinctively put my hand to my forehead. Photographs. We had none. Our entire collection of baby pictures, holiday photos, casual no-special-occasion images, and family albums were gone. And my parents were big picture-takers.

For a moment, I thought that at least we would have the pictures that our grandparents possessed, but then reality returned.

Our grandparents had always enjoyed scrapbooking over picture-taking, saying that they preferred avoiding the digital world if at all possible. While my parents were cheerfully snapping away, Grandma and Grandpa would be making pages and books filled with our baby ultrasounds, certificates of achievement from milestones at school, and cards we gave them on the holidays. I seriously doubted that they even owned a camera.

I felt tears well up in my eyes and in an attempt to distract myself, gobbled down a huge mouthful of peaches. This made me gag slightly. I felt a light tap on my shoulder and jumped as if I had seen a ghost.

"Cool it, Julia. It's just me." I turned around and saw my older brother, Sean, with dark lines under his eyes. He rested his arms on my shoulders for a second, as if to reassure me that it *was* really him and not a spirit, before he went into the pantry and grabbed the can of tomato sauce. Only Sean would consider having plain tomato sauce for breakfast, and expecting him to make a joke about it as he usually would, I was surprised when he remained mute.

As I watched him closely, I saw something in his eyes that made my headache return, something that I had never expected to see in him; his eyes held a look of defeat. It made him barely recognizable.

Sean is one of the strongest people I know. I couldn't think of a time when he hadn't been there for me. I considered just how much these past two weeks had really changed us and I wondered if we would ever truly get back to normal.

Suddenly the image of my younger sister, Danielle, filled my mind. I thought about how she always seemed to feel as if she did not belong with us, which was, of course, completely ridiculous. She had grown apart a few years ago and now rarely spoke to us. I suspected that the many years of people singling her out as the 'different' sibling because of her distinct, yet lovely, looks made her think she was unwanted, unwelcomed. She must have felt like she did not belong, which is a horrible way for a young child to feel. I knew that she loved us though, and I wished deeply that there was some way we could make her feel more like she belonged.

Danielle was close to our parents, as we all were, but since she never quite felt connected with the rest of her siblings, losing Mom and Dad was probably the hardest for her. For the past few days, I had noticed that she had been eating very little and sleeping even less. It was about her that I worried the most out of all my siblings.

Then, abruptly, something happened that brought me back to reality and my hand, full of a spoonful of peaches, headed toward my mouth, froze. Maybe it was luck, or perhaps pre-women's intuition, but in the next moment, I found myself racing toward the guest room that Danielle and TJ had been sharing. I could hear Sean, who took one look at me and sensed something was wrong, sprinting after me. I flung open the door and saw only the sleeping body of my four-year-old brother, sprawled across the bed.

It did not matter that we searched the house a thousand times, opened up the closets, checked the backyard, and woke the others; in our hearts we knew the truth.

Danielle was gone.

Chapter 2

"*I* just don't understand it. Why didn't she come to us if she was this upset? She couldn't seriously have run away, she just couldn't have. Not now. We don't need this right now. Why didn't she come to us?" Mandy was pacing back and forth, hands twitching at her sides.

"Get real Mandy, when is the last time Danielle came to *us* with her problems? I think she would prefer to share them with a talk show host, rather than sit down and have a 'sibling conference,' one where she was actually forced to *talk* to us," Sean replied. His voice had an anxious edge to it.

"Well, where could she be?" Mandy loudly demanded of him.

"How would I know? Quit yelling at me. Gosh you're such a pain."

"How dare you!"

I turned away frantically from my tense older siblings. I had lived with them long enough to sense when a fight was fast approaching and brawls between Mandy and Sean were not uncommon, especially when they were both stressed. But I did not have time to deal with them now.

I debated calling my grandparents' cell phone to see if they had found Danielle while searching the neighborhood, but decided against it. I could not help but hear my gut instinct telling me that their pursuit would be without results.

I ran toward the back porch and flung open the door to check the backyard again. Almost immediately after I got outside, I stopped in my tracks. We had already searched out there ten times and, being a small backyard, there were only so many places in it she could go.

Unless...

I spotted a small wooden shed leaning shakily up against the side of the fence which surrounded my grandparents' yard. Its peeling yellow paint suggested that it, too, along with the many other possessions my grandparents owned, was many years old. I rushed over to it, picturing a tiny girl within, and saw the thick, rusted lock.

I almost shrieked in frustration and began to jangle the lock madly, trying random combinations to no avail. A moment later I stopped, frozen in place, and let the huge lock bang loudly against the side of the shed. If I couldn't open it, surely Danielle couldn't either.

I slumped down to the grass and laid my head on my arm. I knew that when Danielle did something, she did it because she felt she needed to and hiding from her family for no apparent reason did not seem like a realistic motive.

Think Julia, think. I searched my brain and could come to only one conclusion. I jumped to my feet, darted back inside, and made for the front door. Mandy saw me before I reached it and, scooping a sleepy TJ up from her lap on the living room couch, she followed after me, with Sean only a few paces behind her.

Dashing along the sidewalk, I traced the trail back to our parents' house, or what was left of it, a route that was deeply engraved in my mind.

We must have looked peculiar, four frantic-looking children sprinting toward a destination as if their lives depended on it, one of them holding a young child in her arms and the older boy still in his pajamas.

I realized that Mandy must have been tired. TJ is most certainly not light, especially when carried for more than a few minutes. When I looked behind to see how the others were doing, however, I saw TJ, now fully awake and running ahead of the others, obviously delighted to use up some of his energy during this new game.

Soon enough, I saw a familiar mailbox up ahead. I took a deep breath (which was not exceptionally deep since I had been running) and kept on going, steadying my pace and bracing myself for the worst. We had not visited our home since the disaster. I hoped TJ would be all right returning back.

When I came closer, I felt my shallow, short breaths catch in my throat. Near our black mailbox, everything looked strangely normal. The grass was green, the large tree that resided at the foot of our driveway seemed healthy, and the air was ripe with that summer smell. For one fleeting moment, I thought that perhaps it had all been a mistake. I imagined that our parents were alive and well, waiting for us on the porch, as usual.

But then I lifted my head higher and saw the horror beyond that seemingly normal-looking scene.

Nothing. That word had recently been coming into my life more times than I liked.

The place where our house had been was now nothing but a large, black, burnt-colored spot in the middle of scorched grass that had once been our front and back lawns.

I do not know what I had expected. Perhaps some shards scattered around, but not this; this was much worse. It was as if our entire lives had never existed there. As if it had all just been a realistic dream. As if someone had gone back in time and erased all that we had loved and cared for, leaving in its place a black abyss of burnt grass and misery.

I felt sick at the thought of what Danielle might do after confronting this ruin and looked around to tell the others that we must hurry. But when I tried to yell out, I found that I could not speak. I saw blackness forming at the corners of my eyes, creeping forward as I reached out to clutch the mailbox, but missed.

I wondered where Danielle was, and if she was all right.

And then there was darkness.

Nothing, once again.

Chapter 3

"*H*ey look! She's waking up. Guys, c'mere," I heard Sean say, sounding faraway. I pried my heavy eyelids open and saw the faces of my sister and two brothers hovering over me. TJ had his small hands on my head, as if he wanted to transfer his energy into my body. He seemed delighted that it had worked.

Propping myself up unsteadily, I looked up to a high and familiar, yet unidentifiable, ceiling. I still felt slightly faint and wondered if perhaps I was seeing things.

"Jules? Are you feeling okay?" Mandy was staring at me intensely and I could tell that a large number of concerned questions were on her lips, just waiting to leap out and be fired in my direction.

"Yeah, I think I'm fine now," I mouthed a little too quietly.

"What?" She said loud enough to more than make up for my soft response.

"I said I'm fine!" I shouted, unintentionally sounding more annoyed than I actually was.

"Ok, ok, we thought we had lost you for a second when you blacked out back there," Sean replied cautiously. He was probably hoping that he would not get yelled at too.

"Back there..." I murmured, still trying to make heads or tails of what was going on.

"Yes, back there, you must have been really shocked. So we picked you up, and Mandy, you can imagine, was going berserk..."

"Hey, I was not..."

But I was not listening, for I had just spotted a small, curly-haired girl kneeling quietly behind Sean, looking troubled.

"Danielle!" I screamed, crawling toward her on the wooden floor on my hands and knees. When I reached her, I engulfed her in a tight hug and asked the first of many questions that came to my mind.

"Where are we?"

Mandy beamed and, at such a ghastly time as this, I could not for the life of me presume why. She stood up.

"Looks familiar, doesn't it?" she said.

I nodded slowly and she helped me to my feet. She then gripped my arm and led me outside through an opening in the wall of whatever structure we were in.

As we walked down a small set of steps, I stumbled considerably, still a little weak from fainting, but Mandy held me tight. When we reached the bottom and I saw the black emptiness off a little to the right that was once our home, I was afraid that I might get sick again.

But then Mandy turned me around suddenly and I felt a joy that I had not known still existed in me, a happiness I was scared I might have lost forever. A smile broke out on my face, mirroring that of Mandy's before. If at that very minute a passerby would have walked up, from my expression they might have guessed that my parents had returned from the dead.

Directly in front of me was a pure white, freestanding, and miraculously unharmed gazebo. Our gazebo, that resided at the back of our once-cherished backyard. I thought I had never seen anything so beautiful.

Incredibly, after all that had happened, it looked as it always had. Its shingled roof resembled that of a large, opened umbrella. It was surrounded by white poles supporting the sides and a small path of stone steps led up to the entrance. To me, this structure symbolized home.The gazebo filled my mind with memories, but one specifically tugged at my mind. I remembered a time, what seemed like long ago, when I had painted this white structure from a window view. The memory became gradually clearer and the things around me presently transformed into the setting of the flashback. The burnt lawn seemed to disappear before my eyes, and a beautiful room in a lovely house became my new surroundings. I was painting with pastels at a wooden desk, staring out the window at the peaceful white gazebo.

I felt the memory begin to slip away, and tried to hold on to it, to make it last. But soon I was gazing at the structure on the barren lawn once again.

A few years before Mandy was born, my father, William Avery, had built this gazebo for my mother, Christine, for their first wedding anniversary. My father was an architect and had designed and constructed the gazebo by himself. My parents used to love sitting in it, watching the sun set and the stars materialize. Looking at it now, I could see our family in my mind, sipping chilled iced-tea while resting on the soft, cushioned benches.

My eyes drooped slightly, and for the first time since I saw this completely unscathed piece of our previous life, I felt saddened. A warm, steady hand rested on my shoulder and I looked up into Mandy's compassionate eyes. I knew that she understood.

"Danielle was here?" I inquired, trying to keep my voice steady. She nodded, obviously in deep thought.

"She was just sitting quietly inside. We asked her what she was doing here, but she only shook her head and said 'sorry.' We tried to comfort her for a while, but she looked like she wanted to be left alone. This must be really hard for her. I guess she just didn't believe, couldn't believe, that they were really gone until she saw for herself. *I* still can't quite believe it either. It doesn't seem real."

I reached out and took a step forward, touching an edge of the gazebo softly.

"But can you believe it, Jules? It's such a miracle that our gazebo didn't catch fire too. Look, even the grass is burnt almost up to the edge. Somehow it managed to remain unharmed. I swear, it's like a sign," Mandy said.

A sign of what? I wondered, but stayed silent.

She told me that I had been out cold for a few minutes, and they were really worried about me, ready-to-call-911 worried. Knowing Mandy, I believed it.

As she talked, I looked up and saw Sean a little farther away, leaning out over the railing with a cell phone to his ear, no doubt calling Grandma and Grandpa to tell them Danielle had been safely discovered.

Mandy continued to look thoughtful as we made our way back up the steps and sat down on one of the long benches. Sean took a seat again a moment later beside Danielle, who had her eyes closed. He held her hand in a comforting way as he stared up at the ceiling, as if in deep concentration.

Mandy watched TJ playing on the floor; he seemed unaware that this was where our house had been destroyed, being happy only because he was back inside a place he recognized.

I gazed outside at a neighbor's backyard. Two young children, a boy and a girl, were running around in circles, carefree and innocent. I watched with longing, remembering how we were once like that too, untroubled and at ease. For a moment, looking back again at the place where our house had been, I could see my mother in her favorite sunshine-yellow blouse and bright blue jeans, walking through the back door and setting down a pitcher of lemonade on the deck table. She waved at us and disappeared into the house, as the house itself vanished into an unreachable void.

"Oh-h-h my!" Mandy's urgent tone brought me out of my reverie and I saw Sean quickly twist his head in an unnatural way to see what was wrong, producing a painful-sounding *crack*.

"Ouch!" he cried out, but Mandy was not paying attention. She was crawling forward on her hands and knees toward TJ. Her unblinking eyes were on a large object in his grasp. I could not see what it was, for TJ had surrounded it almost entirely with his body. I glanced back at Sean, who was rubbing his neck and complaining.

"What is it this time?" he said hotly, as he rolled his eyes dramatically, probably suspecting this to be one of Mandy's overreactions.

When she reached TJ on the other side of the gazebo floor, she gently pried his fingers off the object he was gripping so tightly. His tiny hands were white from the effort. I was curious now and crouched down to get a better view. I noticed that Danielle's eyes looked like they were bulging out of their sockets.

The hard floorboards had paint that was chipping from age and I lightly brushed off some of the top layer that had tinted my fingers. I inched ahead until I was just a foot or two to the right of Mandy, and that was when I saw it.

I suddenly knew what TJ was so protective of, why Mandy had gasped at the sight, and why Danielle suddenly looked like it was her turn to faint. Tears welled up in my eyes, and I wondered how I could feel so fortunate when we were standing in our house's graveyard.

Chapter 4

I retrieved the large glass jar from a for-once-silent Mandy as Sean ambled up, muttering, "What in the world?"

I slid my fingers against the warm glass, reintroducing myself with all its parts and basking in its profound glory, a glory that only members of our family would recognize. When Sean approached, he too grew hushed as we lifted our heads in unison and gaped at one another in awe.

If this jar that we were clutching so tightly had been sitting on a shelf in a gift shop, customers might glance in its direction and wonder to themselves why anyone would waste money on something so simple and seemingly plain. This is partly true, for it does not look like much. It is merely a glass container, secured tightly with a lid, and filled with multi-colored stones. If one looked closer however, they would notice that between the small stones lay unusual, varied trinkets. What the unknowing shoppers would not realize, however, is that this seemingly meaningless jar represented the special times of our past. The past that we thought we had lost forever.

I can still recall the day, many years ago, when my father had brought a glass jar home after he had been away for a work project in Washington. We had waited excitedly for his return, and when he told us on the phone that he would bring back a surprise, we were doubly eager. When

he walked through the door and produced a plain jar filled
with small glass stones, though, we were more confused
than thrilled. He had set it on the table and told us to rum-
mage around inside to find a stone unlike the rest. We
greedily thrust our youthful hands into the strange jar and
it was Sean who pulled out a rock that was bigger than the
others. On it was a message in red, written by my father in
neat cursive, that read:

The Avery Treasures

My father explained to us how whenever we shared a
memory, really any meaningful memory at all, we would
put a token of that occasion inside the jar. But there were
three conditions. First, it had to be a memory that involved
the entire family. Second, it had to be something that would
make us smile, if not at the time, then later on, when we
looked back on it. Lastly, the jar itself would be kept
indoors during the winter so we could reminisce together
on cold, frosty nights, and kept outdoors during the warm
seasons, within the gazebo, while we enjoyed the beautiful
weather.

Our father had explained to us that with time, we
would truly be thankful that we started a 'memory jar,' as
he referred to it. He told us that he felt that it was an important thing to do to keep the family together and that it
would cheer us up when we were down. And for years
afterward, we did in fact store small keepsakes inside its
glass interior. At first we had gone along with it to please
our father, but as time went on and we grew older, we ourselves began to enjoy the experience as well.

And now, here it was. Our jar full of memories, unin-
jured and glowing.

When I finally found my voice, I realized that I was
unable to think of anything to say. My siblings were equally

quiet, except for TJ, who was singing an unidentifiable song to himself.

I could tell by each of my siblings' faces that they too were overwhelmed with mixed feelings of joy and confusion and amazement all at once. Mostly, though, we were thankful that we now had something that was meaningful to our parents.

"I don't believe it," Sean spoke, his voice barely above a whisper. "What is it doing out here anyway?"

"Don't you remember?" Mandy replied, not looking up. "It's the summertime. Mom must have taken it out here and placed it in the gazebo for the season. Like always..."

I asked TJ where he had found it, and he hastily pointed to a corner. He seemed to be proud that his discovery was causing such a commotion. Sean sat back down on a bench, as if standing up took too much effort.

Though I would still have given anything to have our photo albums back, I realized that this jar had been spared, and for that I felt beyond grateful. I stared at it as memories already began to flood back into my mind, like pieces of a puzzle trying to form a completed picture.

I then heard sniffling, glanced over, and saw Danielle crying in the corner. This made TJ cry as well, and soon, despite our find, wails of sorrow could be heard from the beautiful, white gazebo.

I went over and put my arms around them both, the reminiscences continuing to rush over me. I glanced at Sean, who was now scowling, and Mandy, who was looking sullen. I realized that instead of consoling us, the jar had brought with it a terrible pain. Searching my mind for some way to cheer everyone up, I could find none. I, too, was beginning to feeling quite awful, but forced myself not to show it, for the others' sakes.

Still holding the jar, I sat down in between Danielle and TJ.

"How about we take out some of the keepsakes, like the good old times," I said on a whim, keeping my voice steady. As I unscrewed the top and reached into the container, Sean put his hand on mine to stop me.

"Come on, it can't hurt," I said, knowing very well that it could. "It's for the little ones, Sean." He frowned slightly but dropped his hand.

Not to be deterred, I reached in and dug inside, pulling out a small object clutched in my palm. I wondered for an instant if I was making a mistake, but my body now seemed to be acting of its own accord. Just a second later my right hand opened, revealing my find: a perfectly shaped, pink pearl.

I cleared my throat. "Well, I think I remember the story behind this one. Does anyone want to remind us?"

Silence.

"Okay, fine, I will," I said, a little annoyed that I was the only one willing to help out. I closed my eyes and thought hard.

After a few short moments, I smiled in remembrance. I opened my eyes and was both satisfied and dismayed that I had the attention of everyone. Taking a deep breath and praying that I would not break down, I began the anecdote.

Sandy Pleasure Beach
2 summers back

"Has anyone seen my lucky shark tooth?" 10-year-old Sean yelled from the water up to his mother and sisters who were resting on a blanket on the sand.

"Sean, that is the *least* lucky thing in the world," Mandy shouted back.

"Not true, right after I found it today, I also found five bucks lying next to it," he replied. Sean turned back to the open water and waded in farther.

"Little does he know he found his own money which fell out of his pocket when he bent down to pick up the tooth," the lovely, brown-haired woman next to Mandy whispered, as they bent over in fits of laughter. A few minutes later, a tall, brown-haired man holding hands with a small two-year-old strolled up to the blanket, handing everyone different colored ice cream cones.

"Thanks Daddy," Danielle said as she took a cone from him. Julia, who was beside her, asked her if she liked the flavor, and Danielle gave a small shrug, as if embarrassed.

Sean came up in his bathing suit, sandy from head to foot, a true symbol of the accuracy of the beach's name. He happily received his ice cream. "Well, anyway, if you do find my shark tooth, tell me. I know I put it in my pocket right before we got changed, maybe it—hey!"

He stood up and began chasing a suspicious-looking TJ who had gotten up and ran, dangling a small, but identifiable, object in his tiny grasp. The family watched as the older boy caught the younger one by the shirt and lifted him up teasingly as if he had caught a prize. He walked back over, still holding up his catch, and then set the giggling TJ down. He pried his shark tooth out of the little boy's hand.

"You trickster, you've been playing your little hide-and-seek game all day," Will Avery said while chuckling. "Just this morning, I found my keys in TJ's car seat," he remarked to his wife.

"I guess I now know who took my missing lipstick," their mother said, rolling her eyes jokingly.

"Um, actually Mom, that was me," Mandy said guiltily.

A half hour later, they were all on the water's edge and would be for the remainder of the afternoon. They continued splashing in the ocean and looking for beached sea creatures. The family meandered along, stepping on the wet, hot sand examining anything interesting that they found. Sean fed the rest of his ice cream to a hungry seagull who, afterward, continued to follow him around, begging for more.

The sun rose high in the sky, but the cool water spraying their bodies protected them from the heat. Mandy was trying to teach TJ to float, without the slightest bit of success, when suddenly, toward the late afternoon, Julia gave out a shout and called everyone over.

"Look at this," she exclaimed swiftly, holding up a small object. In her hand rested an opened shell, rather unattractive on the outside, but lying within it was a beautiful, pink pearl.

"Wow," their father said, "look at that." He whistled. "There's a real beauty."

"Where did you find it, Jules?" Sean asked.

"Just here, right on the sand," she replied.

"Do you think it's valuable?" her brother wondered out loud.

"Might be," his father said, "Perfectly symmetric pearls sometimes are. The funny thing is though, I'm pretty sure natural pearls from oyster beds don't turn up around here. It *does* look natural though, very interesting indeed."

"Awesome! A rare, valuable pearl just happens to turn up and we're the ones who find it. What are the odds? See, I knew this shark tooth was lucky," Sean said while whooping with glee.

Mandy rolled her eyes. "We don't know that it's rare or valuable, genius."

Julia was still admiring the pink pearl while her parents talked about possibly taking it somewhere to get it appraised, when TJ began complaining about his hunger. The air was turning cooler, a sure sign of the approaching evening, so the children's parents discussed various places to eat. They finally decided on a pleasant, semi-fancy seafood restaurant about ten minutes from the beach by car.

Before leaving, they sauntered along the boardwalk for a while, playing arcade games, buying souvenirs, and giving their immensely sandy feet a chance to become visible again.

All the while, the children excitedly discussed the pearl. They talked about where it might have originated from, their luck in finding it (courtesy of Sean and his tooth), and how much it might be worth: hundreds, thousands, maybe even a million dollars! The more they talked about it, the more attached to it and animated about it they became.

Later on, they arrived at *The Ocean Mist Hideaway* restaurant and were seated outdoors beneath a large, red awning. From their table, they could see the ocean beyond the deck, and such a wonderful view it was. The sun was beginning to set, turning the sky a collage of beautiful colors, and the water looked peaceful. They could see elegant blue and white boats lined up along the pier.

By this time, they were all famished, having only had ice cream for lunch. They placed the pink pearl inside its shell, closed it so it would stay unharmed, and put it in the middle of the table for safekeeping.

Their father, being a big seafood enthusiast, ordered lobster and a side of fried calamari, while their mother decided on a delectable flounder dish. The children's parents let the children choose whatever they wanted since this was a special daytrip. The two older children both chose shrimp scampi, Julia ordered salmon, Danielle decided on flounder like her mother, and young TJ was satisfied with sharing everyone else's meals. When his father offered him some of his calamari though, the little boy squealed at the thought of eating squid.

When they had finished their delicious meal and paid, they remained seated for a few minutes longer. Sean took out his lucky shark tooth and tied it around a spare piece of string he found on the boardwalk, to form a necklace. TJ, from the other side, watched in toddler-wonder as it swung gently from his hands.

Then, all of a sudden, TJ lurched forward in an attempt to grab it. His mother tried to hold him back while Sean swatted so his brother could not reach the necklace. That was when Mandy and Julia both saw the shell fly into the air, knocked by Sean's swatting or TJ's grabbing. The two girls both pointed and the rest of the family gazed upward. The shell then changed direction and dropped fast toward the ground, plummeting somewhere beneath the table as the family watched, stunned.

Don't worry, they thought, *it will just hit the floor.* But they waited for a 'bang' and instead heard a soft 'splash.' They looked at one another and then bent down. Below their feet was an ordinary floor made of wooden planks, but two of the boards were not perfectly parallel to each other. Instead, there was a small gap between the boards, and beneath the floor was about a two-foot drop, and then the ocean.

"We're above water?" Sean yelled as he scrambled up and ran toward the exit. His father sprinted after him while his wife gathered up the rest of the children. The four kids and their mother got out of the restaurant soon after, and searched for signs of where Sean and Mr. Avery had gone.

It was Mandy who soon spotted them both, their clothes drenched, in the middle of the dock's water, searching frantically for what seemed to be a needle in a haystack.

A few minutes later, they climbed back up onto land, dripping wet.

"We didn't find it," the children's father said, stating the obvious between short breaths.

And they were correct. They did not find it in the water. Actually, they would not find it until they were back in the car, driving home. There, Danielle would spot TJ playing happily with a small gem in his hand. An object that he had slipped out of the shell during dinner when he decided that the pretty, pink pearl would be another one of his hide-and-seek hostages.

Afterward, the family would decide to place the perfect pearl inside their memory jar, and they never did get around to appraising it, as they were happy enough to have it returned to them.

In fact, looking back on it, Sean and his father would think it amusing that they dove into the cold water in search of something that they had had the whole time. And they would laugh. Almost.

Chapter 5

❧

*W*e sat in silence for a few moments, each of us lost in our own thoughts and memories. I thought I heard Danielle whisper quietly to herself, "I remember," but it might have been my imagination.

I'm not sure what I had expected, but some acknowledgment of the existence of our voices would have been nice. Yet everyone, even TJ, remained quiet.

As if by some invisible sign, we all got up and began the passage back to our grandparents' house. On the way out of the gazebo, Danielle grasped the jar and took it with her. I thought I saw her give me a small smile that only I could see, but it might have been a grimace. As if she knew what I was thinking, she suddenly smiled wider; I smiled back. I knew that it was her way of telling me that she was glad about my idea to reminisce with the memory jar, just like we used to with our parents. For the first time in years, I felt like I had truly helped my recluse-feeling sister.

We walked back in single file, much like a group of young children might do in school, with Mandy in the lead, followed by TJ, Sean, Danielle, and finally me trailing after them. No one had said a word since I had finished recounting the memory of Sandy Pleasure. I can admit that I am not always the most talkative person in a conversation, but on this day, I couldn't stand the lack of dialogue. I was beginning to feel embarrassed, wondering what everyone was thinking.

But it was more than that. I was worried that it had not brought us together in our time of need, as I had hoped it would, even though in the beginning I had only been sharing the story to cheer up Danielle and TJ. It seemed like my brilliant idea had only done more damage, except perhaps for Danielle.

The more we walked on, the more I questioned my act; each step made the regret in my heart grow. By the time we were three quarters of the way to our grandparents' home, I was in constant, silent, self-scolding mode. What had I expected, after all? Everyone to burst out in laughter, our grief forgotten, our old selves restored?

It was at this point that I was weakest about my decision to relive one of our memories, and this was perhaps why I gave in so easily to what was about to happen next.

As we neared the house, Sean lagged behind the others and walked beside me for a few minutes. I did not realize that he was going to say anything until he cleared his throat roughly and looked my way.

"Hey, Julia?"

"Yeah?" I asked.

"I know you were trying to help, and I'm sure it might have been good for the younger ones, since they were feeling bad and all, but let's make it a one-time thing, okay?" he said in one breath.

"What do you mean?" I asked automatically, knowing full well what he meant.

"Come on, do you really think there is any point in bringing the past back up? Jules, it's not going to bring Mom and Dad back, you know."

"I realize that," I said truthfully. He stopped in front of me and put up his hands. I could see Danielle lingering ahead, not facing us, but I could tell she was listening to every word.

"Please, Jules. It won't do any good. I just know it won't. It was probably for the best that we left the jar at the gazebo. Let's just try and get on with our lives, okay? I'm only trying to do what I think is best for all of us."

I knew then that he had not seen Danielle take the jar. I considered telling him, but quickly decided against it.

"Please, no more. I know it's hard, but let's just put it all behind us. No more gazebo, no more trinkets, no more feeling sorry for ourselves. We've got to be strong," he pleaded.

I saw the pain in his eyes and decided that I had been wrong. I should not have brought back up painful memories that had been left at rest. It was only a reminder of what we had lost. I could tell how hard this was for him and knew Sean would not ask this of me unless he felt sure.

"Okay," I said, "no more." He smiled then at me, but the smile was sad. We jogged to catch up with the others as they made their way up the driveway and I noticed that Danielle was already inside the door, having quickly run ahead of us.

Inside the house, our grandparents were engulfing Danielle in a huge embrace, begging her to never run away again, and she agreed hastily, not bothering to tell them that she had not run away. I felt sure that she had every intention of returning to us.

We meandered into the kitchen to help prepare lunch, but I followed Danielle when she swiftly left, heading in another direction. She drifted toward the front hall, retrieving the jar from behind the coat rack where she had hidden it, and quietly ascended the stairs. She must have known that I was tagging along silently, but she made no move to tell me that she wanted to be alone.

Upstairs, in the guest room she shared with TJ, she placed the jar, which held the pearl and many other memories of our parents, gently behind her pillow. Then she lay down on the bed and stared at the ceiling.

I crawled in beside her, and together, we looked up at the white ceiling.

I was surprised at how awful I felt. Despite my previous regret, which had been deep, I couldn't help but feel that I had agreed to Sean's request too quickly. We had found the only thing left that belonged to our past, and now we were going to shut it out of our lives.

I thought about what Mandy had said about the standing gazebo being a sign. That the memory jar had been inside it, and hadn't burned in the fire, seemed to emphasize it. It was like the gazebo had been built to be a safe haven, to protect the jar and show us where it was. And now we were turning our backs on it.

I supposed it was the only way we would be able to move on, but though my mind agreed with Sean, my heart told me otherwise.

I wondered what Mandy thought about it all. She hadn't expressed her opinion on the way back, a rarity for her.

I still felt that somehow, it was almost as if we were meant to rediscover our memories. That perhaps Dad had known that if anything happened that made us feel like we couldn't go on, we might still have the special remembrance jar that we kept for so many years and poured our hearts and souls into. And just maybe that simple-looking jar could help us live again.

But we had no parents, no pictures, and now to our memories as well, we were saying good-bye.

Part 2

Reminiscing

Chapter 6

*T*he next day, a Sunday, I woke up at a late hour, unusual since I am ordinarily a morning person. I had had trouble going to sleep the night before, spending much of the night constantly changing my position and alternating between above and below the covers. My body refused to relax and I desperately yearned for the comfort of my old bed. At one point during the night, I had slipped quietly to the bathroom and did eighty jumping jacks in an attempt to tire myself out. It must have worked, because I did not remember anything after that.

I watched cartoons with TJ for two hours before Mandy came in and insisted that I get ready for the day. Even then, however, it took me a half hour longer to gather up enough motivation to get dressed. I had a feeling that this day would not be one of my better ones.

Mandy, from what I could see, was not doing all that great herself. I saw her try, but fail, to give TJ a bath. Instead, she became soaked when he decided that it was time for *her* to get clean and poured a full cup of his bath water on her head. He then refused to get dressed, preferring to run around the house for twenty minutes, screaming in his underwear.

Danielle had gone to sit outside alone on the front steps that led up to the house and Sean, even at 11:00 in the morning, could still be found fast asleep in his room, his door closed tightly.

Thankfully, Grandma had gone shopping the day before, so our food selection had greatly improved. We were at least able to say that we had a decent breakfast.

Our grandparents had gone out to run a few errands, and as usual, Mandy was in charge. She suggested that we all do a fun craft together to put us in a better mood, but I could tell that she was praying we would decline. Which we did.

At noon, Mandy went to wake Sean up, while I sat down and tried to occupy a disheartened and fidgety TJ. Mandy and I were both ineffective.

For the rest of the day, I let Mandy handle TJ, and closed myself in our room with a book, looking like I was reading. I say from experience that time ticks by rather slowly when you stare at pages unseeingly, turning them repetitively every 57 seconds.

That night, I again had trouble falling asleep. I dreaded another night like the one before and didn't think I had the spirit to do more bathroom exercises. I thought about the next day, which would be the first day of July, and made a resolution not to repeat another day like the previous one. I did not think I would be able to handle it again. A few hours later, I finally fell asleep, dreaming of pearls, jars, and a lone child, lost, scared, and by herself.

I awoke to the beeping sound of the alarm clock, which I had set the night before, determined to get back to my daily routine. I took a long, hot shower, woke TJ up while he was still slightly asleep so he would cooperate, helped him get dressed, and positioned him in front of the television with toast and butter. Afterward, I set the table while Mandy, who seemed persistent as well to make this day better than the last, made everyone eggs and pancakes.

We both woke up Danielle gently and hauled Sean out of his room before he could protest. We then turned the inside lock of his room and shut the door on our way out, so he could not sneak back in. This would prove to be a problem when he tried to go to bed that night.

We were ready for anything.

We were off to a great start and felt that the rest of the day would be a breeze.

We were wrong.

After breakfast, the Avery children were back on the couch, looking bored, restless, and depressed. We stayed that way until our grandmother suggested we take advantage of the beautiful weather and have a picnic for lunch, just the five of us.

I still had my doubts, but it was Mandy who eventually convinced us that a day out might do us some good. Sean and TJ were put on sandwich duty, preparing two ham, one turkey, one peanut butter and jelly, and one peanut butter and fluff sandwich, our favorites. Danielle took care of gathering paper plates, cups, utensils, and napkins, while Mandy and I searched the house for a suitable picnic basket which we found at the back of a closet, slightly dusty, but otherwise in good condition.

It was a beautiful, large basket, another one of those spectacular old-fashioned things that could always be found in my grandparents' house. It had a braided wooden exterior, a sturdy handle, and a red and white cloth inside.

We seemed to all be so caught up with our tasks that we forgot to be irritable. For a while, we even seemed like our old selves again.

A half hour later we piled into our grandparents' car to head out to the local park when we realized that we were missing two items essential to our family picnic: Danielle and the picnic basket. So Sean yelled for her to hurry up.

"Coming!" she said loudly, as she rushed out of the house, basket in hand. I wondered for an instant why she was delayed, but it was quickly dismissed from my mind as we headed off.

Our grandparents dropped us off and told us they would be back to pick us up in an hour and a half. The park, which we had been visiting regularly for a few years now, was, as always, absolutely stunning. Huge trees blossomed over fresh, green grass and a sparkling lake. To the right of the main entrance was a spot dedicated to the widest variety of flowers I have ever seen: lilies, lilacs, petunias, roses, daisies, sunflowers, pansies, carnations, all positioned expertly together so as to appear full and beautiful, yet not too crowded. The park was not too busy today, despite the perfect weather, and there were plenty of spots available for eager picnickers.

We found a shady area under a large black walnut tree and began to set up. I was pleased to see that everyone, including myself, seemed to be in good spirits. Mandy and I laid out the blanket and Sean handed TJ the items from within the basket.

Suddenly, though, he stopped short and his pleasant smile was immediately wiped off his face. Out of the basket he pulled the memory jar.

Chapter 7

*S*ean looked my way accusingly.

"Julia, you promised. How could you take it out of the gazebo? Are you trying to upset us all?" He was red in the face and it seemed as if just holding the jar caused him severe pain.

I saw Danielle look surprised that Sean had addressed me reprovingly, instead of her, and she caught my eye before bending her head with shame.

Though I admit that despite the many mystery novels I have read, I can barely qualify as an amateur detective, at that instant, based on numerous clues, a few things became clear to me.

Danielle wanted to hear more stories. I wondered if that was as bad a thing as Sean was making it out to be, and decided that retelling memories of happier times in periods of sorrow, did not seem that awful at all. And at that point, I would have done just about anything to help Danielle.

But why did it bother Sean so? I had trusted my brother, like I always did, when he told me that stopping the stories was for the best of us all, but perhaps he himself did not realize that what he was asking me to do was, in reality, for himself.

I knew enough about Danielle to understand that having Sean put her on the spot, unfairly, and scold her in front of everyone would be nothing less then disastrous. And I was willing to make the sacrifice.

"Yes, it was me," I said, "and no, I'm not trying to upset anyone."

Danielle looked up, a confused expression on her face. Sean was yelling in the background, but I was not really listening. I was looking at my little sister as she smiled at me. The smile was for once, in longer than I could remember, not held back at all, nor was it anything but true. It was one of the most beautiful, purest smiles I had ever seen.

She knew I took the blame for her. She had not expected me to and I had, just because I loved and cared for her and now she was sure of that. For the first time, she really understood what it felt like for a big sister to take care of her younger sister; she felt secure.

"Julia! Are you listening to me? Are you paying any attention at all?" Sean looked close to tears. I could tell he was extremely angry with me, and I knew he thought I had hurt him.

I did not know what to do, so I stood there mutely and, although I was glad I had protected Danielle, I wasn't feeling on top of the world at that particular moment. I had always hated being yelled at and Sean and I hardly ever fought with each other. If anything, he had been the one who was usually on my side.

But then, like an angel appearing to spread joy, or a mother emerging to defend her young, I heard Mandy's voice through the gloom. It was as if all her silence on the topic from the past two days had finally grown too much to handle and burst out of her, forcing its way through her mouth, aimed directly at Sean.

"Stop it," she said sternly. I could tell this was going to be different from their usual, petty arguments. Her tone immediately brought him to a halt, mid-sentence.

"Mandy…"

"No, Sean. Now, I am not exactly sure what is going on here, but I know one thing for certain. It seems to me that you are deciding how everyone should feel about the memory jar yourself. Have you ever thought that maybe we don't feel the same way as you do?"

"Well—"

"And have you ever asked *me* what I thought about it? You assumed that you knew. And do you know what? You assumed wrong. I thought it was a great idea when Julia told us the story, and I feel no differently now. I'll admit that at first, it was hard to hear about the ones we love and have lost, but it also does a lot of good. You can't spend the rest of your life avoiding the past. It is a part of you and forever will be. We all have to learn to heal, but *forgetting* about our parents and all the good times we had with them is not the answer. It's not what Mom and Dad would have wanted us to do."

Sean was speechless.

"I know what I'm talking about Sean, trust me I do. After all, I am the oldest." She smiled at me.

Sean must have sensed that his opinions were overshadowed for he turned away and stared into the distance, for once not bothering to continue a fight with Mandy, perhaps knowing that he had already lost. Though part of me wished I could go over and comfort him like he had done for me so many times, I also knew that Mandy's words were something that he had to hear.

"Now, I think it's time we heard another story," she said, "What was the point of saving all those keepsakes if we don't even use them at the time we need them the most, after all. Besides, I think it's about time we reminded TJ of his childhood with his parents, before he forgets, that is," her voice cracked slightly. "Does anyone disagree? Good, but this time if you don't mind, I'd like to have a go at one." She reached for the jar and after digging inside for a few seconds, pulled out a red ribbon with the words 'Johnny's Fish Bowl Toss' written in gold.

"Okay, hmmm. Now let's see," she began confidently. "It was a sunny Saturday afternoon in the late fall. We were all so excited when we found out that a carnival-type fair was coming, not too far away from our house..."

Travis Town Fair
4 years back

The catchy carnival music could be heard from a mile away and walking around the fair with the lights flashing, rides twirling, and the melodies in the background could almost be too much excitement for one young child to bear, or in this case, five young children.

The first attraction that caught young five-year-old Danielle's eyes, however, was the fish bowl toss stand. The mechanism behind it is quite simple: the thrower is given a set of three ping pong balls which they toss into small, plastic fish bowls, resting on a hard surface. Some of the bowls have bright, red rims, and if the thrower is able to throw the balls into these bowls, then he or she can take home the prize of a new pet fish.

Danielle found this whole concept quite thrilling and, after begging her parents, the family decided to stop by that stand first. Her mom and dad paid the dollar fee and Danielle retrieved her three balls. The first one she threw bounced off the edge of a bowl at the very end, and rolled under the Ferris Wheel a few feet away. The second one hit the stand's worker hard on his bald head. The third, however, made it into a bowl, but unfortunately not one of the red-rimmed ones. Danielle pleaded with her parents for one more go before moving on, so they bought three more balls. Danielle wanted that fish so badly, it would be her first pet after all. It might have been determination or perhaps it was merely pure luck, but after just one more throw, Danielle made it into a red-rimmed bowl and was able to get a fish.

A cute little fish was given to her in a transparent bag, tied closed with a red ribbon labeled with the name of the fish stand in gold.

And did she ever love that fish.

She held it proudly in the air, letting strangers admire it, and gently talked and cooed to it as they continued their stroll through the fair. Danielle knew right away what she would name the fish, and that was Fishy Fish: Fishy being the fish's first name, and Fish being its last name, as she smartly pointed out. She had given this quite a lot of thought.

The family of seven stopped at a blue stand to get cotton candy and snow cones. They then rested under a pavilion for a few minutes, eating, and feeding baby TJ his bottle while he sat contentedly in his stroller.

It was Sean who soon spotted an awe-inspiring ride called the Whirlwind Rush. It was a medium-sized attraction that had ten different colored house-shaped structures protruding out of its base, which spun around while riders sat inside the 'houses.' Then, the houses themselves were turned upside down a few times before setting the riders back safely on the ground.

"Will, I'm not sure this looks safe for the kids," the children's mother said worriedly. The worker assured them, however, that the ride was safe for children five and over, for it did not go very fast.

"Awesome," was all a young Sean could say from delightful anticipation.

Mandy and Sean boarded the ride hurriedly, while Julia preferred staying with her parents.

"Seven years old is an awfully young age to die," was all she had stated when they had asked her to come along.

Danielle, however, wanting to be like her older brother and sister, decided to ride along with them.

Their mother watched in agitation as the ride began and the children were flipped and spun, turned and shook up, and it seemed ages to her until they finally landed. She ran to the miniature houses, ready to provide comfort, but found instead an air of excitement and shouts of wanting to ride again. Their mother thought she might faint.

It was not until a few minutes later, as they were walking toward a game booth, that Danielle said cheerfully, "I think he's sleeping."

"Who, honey?" Danielle's mother asked.

"Fishy."

They all stopped and looked at Danielle's small, plastic bag that had once held a healthy-looking goldfish. Now though, Fishy was lying on his back, his vacant eyes staring straight ahead, his body floating at the top.

"I guess Fishy just wasn't Whirlwind Rush material," Sean muttered to Mandy, who flicked his head.

They watched as Danielle stroked the see-through bag, and said in a hushed voice, "I'll see you when you wake up Fishy Fish."

They all felt bad about Danielle's fish, but it was Julia and Sean who felt the worst. After convincing their parents that they would be just fine by themselves, they decided to go back to the fish toss to win her another one.

Mr. and Mrs. Avery gave their two children three dollars and dropped them off at the booth. They told them for the tenth time that they would just be a few feet away, at the boat rides. The children's mother kept on glancing back to see how they were doing, as her husband continued to assure her that they would be okay.

At the boat ride, the small boats were in the shape of ducks, complete with a green head, yellow bill, and brown body.   Mandy and Danielle climbed into one of the boats as the worker, a twenty-something-year-old man with blond hair, explained to them how to operate it.

"Okay, now since you are the older one, you will do the pedaling. It's just like a bicycle, so don't worry, it's easy.

And this lever here, you pull it *right* when you want to go left and *left* when you want to go right. Now make sure you don't crash into anyone, or anything for that matter. Okay? Okay. Now have fun!"

But the young girls were so excited that they had barely paid attention. The man gave them a big push and they were off, their parents and TJ in another boat off to their right, heading in the opposite direction. For a few moments they drifted here and there, still continuing from the force of the man's strong push, but after a little while, they drew to a halt.

"What do we do now?" Danielle asked.

"Er, I think I'm supposed to pedal," replied Mandy, as she turned her feet in a circular motion. But they were heading straight for another boat, so Mandy yelled to Danielle, "Quick, use the lever and turn right."

"Which way's right?" Danielle wondered out loud.

"That way." Mandy pointed. Danielle pulled the lever the way her sister was pointing, but the boat began to turn the opposite way from the way that she was pulling, heading them straight toward the other boat.

Meanwhile, back at the fish-toss station, Sean and Julia had paid for and received nine balls.

"Now, let's see who the better thrower is," Sean said to Julia. "You try first." Julia threw a ball and it missed drastically. Then Sean threw a ball and his made it into one of the regular-rimmed bowls.

"I think you're a bit better than me," Julia said.

So Sean continued to throw the balls one by one, but though he made it into a regular bowl a few times, he never came close to one of the red-rimmed ones, and soon all their balls were used up.

"Great, now what do we do?" Julia moaned.

"It's okay, I brought my allowance money. I'm sure I'll get it in one of these times." He held up ten dollars.

"Ahhhh!" Mandy and Danielle screamed in chorus as they missed yet another duck boat by an inch.

"How do you work this thing, Mandy?" Danielle screeched over Mandy's continued yelling.

"If I knew that, I wouldn't be screaming, would I?" They pulled the lever right and left and continued going in all sorts of mixed-up directions, none of them the way in which they intended to go.

Suddenly, Mandy spotted a patch of land directly in front of them.

"Oh, no! We're going to crash!" Danielle squealed.

"Wait a second," Mandy said thoughtfully, and stopped pedaling. Right as she ceased, the boat stopped moving altogether.

"Oh," they said in unison.

"How did Danielle *do* it?" Sean exclaimed loudly.

"I don't know, but how much money do you have left?" Julia inquired.

"About, oh no, only 2 dollars!"

Sean spotted a red-rimmed bowl off to the far left that he had not tried for yet and stared at it intensely. Then he bent his arm back, exhaled, and let the little ball fly.

It landed smack dab in the middle of the red-rimmed bowl.

"Woo-hooooo!" Sean howled joyfully as Julia patted him on the back in congratulations.

"I can't wait to show Mandy and Mom and Dad," he said.

"What's all the commotion about?" the children's father asked, as he pulled up his own boat next to his daughters' boat.

"Dad!" they both said, relieved.

"See, Will! I told you they were too young. I barely understand how to work this thing myself," their mother said.

"Don't worry guys, we're here now. Can you ride the boat back with TJ?" he asked his wife.

"I think so, but why?"

"I'm going to ride back with them," their father said.

"Are you crazy? You can't switch boats in the middle of the lake. You won't be able to make it!" replied his wife.

"Is that a challenge?" he said, and chuckled. "Don't worry, now let me pull our boat up close to theirs."

"Be careful."

Will Avery began to reach forward and step onto his children's boat, and he probably would have made it flawlessly if he had not heard something that caught him off guard.

"Sir, we cannot allow you to change boats in the middle of the water," yelled the blond-haired worker deafeningly, his voice loud from a megaphone.

Their father gave a yelp at this unexpected distraction and fell forward, reaching out his hands.

And as their mother feared, there they were: two duck boats, one containing two children and the other with a mother and her young baby, and in between them, stretched out, was a man, his hands clutching one boat, and his feet propped up against the other.

Christine frantically pulled her boat up closer, for it had gotten pushed away during the struggle, and her husband was able to safely climb aboard, though not avoid his wife's heated stare.

When they got back to land, Julia and Sean were waiting. Then, on cue from Sean, Julia slipped the fish bag away from Danielle and traded it with Sean's new one.

"Look Mommy, Fishy woke up. I knew he would." Danielle shouted happily as Sean grinned. "But Mommy, how did his red ribbon change to blue?"

Chapter 8

*A*t first there was a haunting silence, and I was reminded of the quiet that had also been present after the pearl story. I was not sure what to say, so instead stared reluctantly into the expressionless faces of my siblings. Then suddenly there came a sound that was as genuine as music and it was welcomed graciously by my ears.

Danielle burst out laughing.

Mandy and I stared at one another in astonishment, and then we, too, began giggling uncontrollably. Pretty soon we were clutching our stomachs, rolling on the grass, and wiping tears from our eyes. It was the first time I had laughed since the disaster.

"Are you kidding me? You switched my fish? He was dead? I never even knew," Danielle stated between giggles. I think it was one of the longest sentences I had heard her speak to us in a year.

We began to pack up our lunch, still smiling. Our grandparents would be here soon. I knew what I was feeling, and I suspected everyone else was feeling the same thing: like we were part of a family again. I hoped the sensation would last as I folded up the blanket and supported it under my arm. I held one end of the basket while Mandy took hold of the other. Danielle picked up TJ, who had fallen asleep during the story, and Mandy joked about how he had nodded off because of the boring way she told it.

It was then that I looked around and noticed that someone was missing. Mandy read my thoughts.

"Yeah, I saw Sean leave toward the end. Guess he wanted to walk home alone."

I saw Danielle, who was still smiling gently, suddenly grow serious, thinking.

"I never knew that he spent all his allowance on me, just for me to be happy," she said softly.

We headed toward a silver mini van that had just drawn to a halt at the curb. As we drove home, I thought about Sean.

Avoidance. That was my brother's way of dealing with grief. He must have been hurting inside more than any of us knew, hurting more than he let on. Sean in particular had always been the one that I leaned on in hard times, but I knew that this time he truly needed us as well.

But I also felt that avoidance was not the answer, and I wished that there was some way I could make him understand that too.

When we arrived at Grandma and Grandpa's house, my grandmother called me into the living room and took out one of her scrapbooks, entitled 'My Sunshines.' We sat down together and I ran my hand across the book's hard, brown cover. The first page we opened to had a brochure from a play Mandy was in when she was in sixth grade. On the opposite side was a collection of essays that I had written, along with one that had won a contest and was published in a local newspaper.

We looked at page after page and oddly, I did not feel as sad thinking about the past as I thought I would. Instead, I felt much the same comfort I had experienced when I listened to Mandy tell the story. I was grateful that we had so many great memories as a family that we could share, and I knew that those memories were something I would hold on to forever.

"I want to tell you something, sweetheart. I want you to know that I'm so very sorry that we don't have pictures of your parents for you. I feel like we've failed you and I hope that someday, you will be able to forgive us," my grandmother said in a raspy voice.

"Oh, Grandma," I said, leaning into her, "you've already helped us more than you know."

I followed Mandy into the enclosed glass sunroom about an hour before dinner time, and we worked on putting together a puzzle of a dog with TJ, much to his delight. Danielle joined us a few minutes after we got there, and we all sat together, warm from the sun shining through the glass walls.

This room had always been my favorite spot in my grandparents' house. It was decorated with French Country furniture painted a pearly white, and its walls were covered with quilts of every imaginable color, my grandmother's pride and joy. In the middle of the small room was a table, and on top of it rested a beautiful, large orchid that my grandparents nurtured.

If I had to guess ahead of time who would be next to suggest taking out the memory jar, I might have presumed it would be anyone but TJ. But of course, TJ it was.

"Uh, I think let's do the jar," said TJ's squeaky, happy voice as he matched a piece in the puzzle.

"What, TJ?" Mandy asked, not really paying attention. She was concentrating on finding the piece that would complete the dog's left paw.

"Let's do the jar!" TJ yelled, climbing into her lap, and putting his hands on each of her cheeks. Mandy looked at Danielle, Danielle looked at me, and I said, "Well, what are you waiting for? You heard the man."

Two minutes later, the jar was in the middle of my lap. I reached around inside while the others watched me keenly. I pulled out a shiny souvenir penny. Its face was pressed with a symbol of a light bulb, the famous representation of the concept of thinking and ideas. I cleared my throat and began the story.

"It was a sunny Sunday and not having any specific plans, Mom and Dad decided to take us to a museum that was recommended to them by a friend. The first exhibit we went to was really interesting and it involved..."

"No, no, that's not how it goes," I heard a familiar voice say.

We all looked up to see who had interrupted and saw a skinny, brown-haired boy leaning against the wall of the entrance to the sunroom, hands folded at his chest.

No one seemed to be sure of what to say, or what to expect, as Sean walked toward us. He bent down beside me, took the penny from my hand rather brusquely, and sat down between Danielle and Mandy.

"Don't you think it's my turn to have a go? Well, I remember this one clearly," he stated, then suddenly broke out in a wide smile.

I beamed back at him, knowing that from now on, we were all in this together and everything would be all right.

The Journey To Knowledge Museum
5 years back

Eight-year-old Mandy stared up at the building's sign that read 'The Journey To Knowledge Museum,' tilting her umbrella back as the rain poured down in bucketfuls around her.

"Come on," Sean shouted from the dry inside. Mandy ran through the door that he held open for her and hung her coat on a long rack. She took young Danielle, at four years old, by the hand, and they caught up with their parents at the ticket line.

The front hall of the museum was immense. On the floor was an engraving of a shining light bulb, and hanging from the top of the building were numerous brains that looked strangely realistic. Tall beams ran up from the floor to the ceiling above, curving to form a huge arc at the doorway of the first exhibit room.

"Cool," Sean said, staring at the brains, while Julia, who was just beginning to learn how to read, stared at several signs on the wall in deep concentration, as if their meaning would magically transfer into her head. Sean went over to her and pointed out the different letters and their names, showing off his impressive reading skills.

The six of them, for the youngest Avery child had not yet been born, ambled through the curved entrance a few minutes later. To the children, the room was very much like a completely different world.

Hands-on exhibits covered every inch of the tremendous room. The four children each ran in different directions: Mandy was fascinated with a microscope station in which the looker could inspect various insects and fabric material cells. Sean was drawn to the dinosaur area where he could dig up fossils from a sand pit. Julia went straight over to a painting section where she could mix different colors to create new ones. Danielle ran back and forth between her older siblings, as well as the many displays that caught her interest.

The children tried each exhibit numerous times, running around as if they only had a minute to do them all.

When their parents finally convinced them that it was time to move on, they were all quite gloomy as they thought about all the fun they were leaving behind. Soon however, the bright colors of the next room with a completely different set of exhibits came into view, and the process began all over again.

The second building of the museum was not connected to the first and the only way to reach it was by walking outside. Luckily, the rain had cleared and the family followed a red stone path with tiny yellow light bulbs lining the trail's edges.

They were halfway to the other side when Julia shouted excitedly, "A bee, a b-e-e-e-e-e!"

Everyone looked around.

"Where, honey?" her mother asked, concerned. The children's father had bad bee allergies and rushing to the hospital was not the way the family preferred to spend the rest of their afternoon.

Julia pointed, but for some reason, she seemed oddly excited and was jumping around wildly, making it impossible to spot where she was gesturing. The Avery family began running frantically to the other building, swatting madly at an insect that they could not see, until Sean, who was in front, stopped in his tracks. Everyone else knocked into him.

He looked up, and then at the direction where Julia was pointing, and began laughing hysterically. He pointed also, and everyone looked up at a huge banner, reading:

BUTTERFLY EXHIBIT—Coming Soon!

"A bee!" young Julia said happily, pointing at the first letter of the banner. "Just like Sean showed me. The letter B!"

The first thing the family saw when they opened the gigantic, heavy doors of the next building was a beautiful fountain in the shape of a dancing young girl in a flowing dress, covered entirely with exotic flowers. The children begged their parents for spare change to throw into the fountain, and after digging around in their pockets, Will and Christine gave them some money.

They each made a wish and threw in their coins, relishing the *clink* they made as the money hit the stone bottom. Soon the children turned back to their parents, begging for more, and sounding as if their lives depended on it.

This continued a time or two longer, until Mr. and Mrs. Avery had run out of dimes, nickels, and pennies, and it was then that they were finally able to convince the children to continue on their way.

The exhibits in the second building were just as spectacular as those in the first. There were sections on ancient cultures, dinosaurs, and the human body, with life-like figurines and fascinating information at each and every display.

The last section they visited was the Wax Room, a miniature wax museum filled with realistic-looking people that children, as well as their parents, would recognize. The room was empty except for the Avery family and they were glad to have the space to themselves. The children were amazed at the convincingly real figures, such as Dorothy, the Tin Man, the Wicked Witch, the Cowardly Lion, and the Scarecrow from the Wizard of Oz, Mr. Rogers, Elvis, Benjamin Franklin, George Washington, and Shirley Temple.

In the middle of the Wax Room was a penny souvenir machine that flattened pennies and pressed designs into them as a memento. When the family reached it, the children's mouths dropped open at this incredible machine.

Will and Christine searched their pockets, but although they were able to locate the two quarters needed to start the mechanism, they were unable to find a single penny, having used up all their spare change casting wishes at the fountain.

Sean began to avidly search the floor by the wax figures' feet, and Mandy checked the pockets of her other siblings. Soon, however, they could not deny the reality of their situation: they had absolutely no change left. To distract the children from their disappointment, their father continued admiring the other wax figures with them and pointed out people they knew.

The final wax figurine was a portrayal of a police officer, dressed professionally in a blue uniform and complete with a sparkly badge.

"Do you recognize this guy?" the children's father asked his wife. She shook her head.

"I can't imagine why they would make a wax figure of an ordinary policeman. Hmmm," he said, puzzled, inspecting the officer closely. "It doesn't even look like they did that great of a job on him either."

"Dad, are you *sure* you don't have any pennies? All we need is one," Sean asked for the thousandth time in a whiny voice.

"I have one, young man. You can have it," said the wax policeman. Will Avery nearly jumped out of his socks as the figure beside him came to life, and reached into his pocket, pulling out a shiny new penny.

"Sorry, I couldn't help myself when I saw that you thought I was made of wax. But trust me, I'm just a regular officer, on duty guarding the exhibits. I'm all flesh and bones." He chuckled.

Sean thought he then heard the officer murmur, "Gets them every time."

When their father seemed to recover from the shock, he burst out laughing, and the rest of the family joined in. Then the children ran to the machine, chose a design, and got their souvenir penny after all.

Chapter 9

*A*fter an enormous dinner of roast beef, creamed corn, tomato soup, and Caesar salad, we kissed our grandparents goodnight and headed up to bed early.

I helped TJ get dressed, and the others put on their bedtime clothes while Mandy put together a plate of dessert snacks and brought it upstairs. We assembled in the room Mandy and I shared, our father's old one, all sitting comfortably on the bed. The jar rested in the middle of our sibling union.

Then together, we talked into the night.

We were truly a family.

At times we would take out some of the trinkets, pass them around, and hold them in our hands, remembering the good times. We told the stories behind them, laughing and crying, comforting and smiling. There were many objects in the jar, more than the night allowed to be told in one sitting. But there would be other times for that, the rest of our lives in fact.

At other points we would discuss anything at all that came to our minds. It was as if everything that had been bottled up inside us refused any longer to be hidden away, unshared.

For a while, it even seemed as if nothing bad had happened, like it was any other summer's day. As if our parents were just across the hall.

For the first time in a very long time, Danielle did not hold back at all. She was soon laughing and chattering along with everyone else. Sean and Mandy were at first surprised and seemed slightly unsure of how to react to the new transformation of our younger sister. After just a few moments, however, it felt natural and right. I was glad that she finally understood that she wasn't alone in this world.

TJ seemed to be enjoying himself as well, talking, eating, laughing, and of course occasionally running around the room. TJ plus dessert equals energy galore.

I thought about the memories we shared as a family, adventures being a better term. It was those little things—spending weekends together, laughing at ourselves and the funny things we'd done, and caring enough about each other to keep tokens of our time together—that truly mattered in the end.

We all felt it, the connection. I understood then that each of us was bonded not only by our memories, but also by the love we had for one another. And that was a bond that could not be broken. We were now renewed, a renewal that had been spurred by a link from our past.

But there was something else as well. Our parents had always stressed family togetherness, but now we seemed closer than ever. I wondered how it was possible that something so horrible and so tragic as the disaster that left the five of us parentless could also have some positive effect. We were now together, and nothing was going to tear us apart.

The next morning, I woke up first and found my head slumped across Mandy's back. I quietly got up off the bed and observed the pile of siblings lounged on top of one another. I couldn't help but smile.

I eyed TJ, curled up at the foot of the bed, and a problem that I often thought about crept into my thoughts. I did not know for sure how much he understood about what had happened. For all I knew, he might have merely thought that our parents were away, and would be back eventually. I worried about him, for despite all his energy he still seemed to me so fragile and innocent in his youthfulness.

At the same time though, I realized that we would be there, always, to care for him. Especially now that we were a family again.

Family. I liked the way that word sounded.

I lay back down on the bed and put my arm around my little brother.

An hour or two later, we were all up and about, ready for a late breakfast, and it was during our brunch that Danielle suggested we go back to the gazebo.

We walked there slowly as a group and entered this time through the back of the property, so as not to have to tread over the burnt grass. At one point, I heard Danielle whimper and I put my arm around her.

But when we reached the inside of the beautiful gazebo, any distressing thoughts we might have had receded into the shadows. I realized that this was the way our parents would have wanted us to feel.

I felt a hand on my shoulder and turned to face Danielle as she placed the jar, which she had taken along, on my lap. Then she reached inside and pulled out a small, orange, pumpkin-shaped button.

"It's about time I had a turn, isn't it?" she said quietly, smiling tenderly.

Pumpkin Acres
1 year back

Eight-year-old Danielle felt the chilly wind rush over her hair wildly and uncontrollably. She did not even bother laying it back down neatly on her head, knowing that in a minute, the next breeze would toss it back again. Her mother beside her took her hand and squeezed it gently as she carried Danielle's three-year-old brother on her hip. They walked across the pumpkin field toward Danielle's father, her older brother, and her two sisters, who were deep in concentration on their task: finding a pumpkin worth picking.

This was an Avery family tradition: going to Pumpkin Acres, a local farm, which was open during the fall months, when grew pumpkins big and ripe, ready for picking. With Halloween fast approaching, the Averys wanted a flawless pumpkin for carving.

"I found one! I found one!" TJ shouted to his dad. He led his father toward one that was shriveled up, an odd shade of orange-green.

TJ was gloomy that his pumpkin was not chosen to obtain the title of, 'The Most Wonderful Pumpkin of the Whole Year.' He was, however, cheerful when he was chosen to be the judge, deciding between either Mandy's or Sean's pumpkin, and his spirits were quickly restored.

A few minutes later, the family walked toward the farm's main building to weigh Mandy's pumpkin, while Sean tickled TJ and questioned why *his* had not been good enough.

After leaving their pumpkin in the barn to be picked up later, they took a short hayride to the farm's food store. Julia, Mandy, TJ, and Sean fussed over the numerous desserts—chocolate scones, sugary muffins, freshly baked cookies, pumpkin pies, and every flavor of cake conceivable, while Danielle was delighted over the homemade apple cider. After buying a cookie for each child, along with two cups of spiced cider to share, a barrel of fresh apples, and a pie for after dinner, the family set off again and caught the next hayride.

Their next stop was the petting area, and a half second after the vehicle halted, the children sped toward the many goats, horses, rabbits, and the single cow. They enjoyed stroking the soft fur of the rabbits, feeling the sticky tongue of the goats as they searched for food crumbs, and petting the beautiful manes of the horses. But while the others busily played with those animals, Danielle was fascinated by the cow.

It was a huge creature with a mostly black head, expect for one small white spot around its right eye. Danielle adored the cow from the moment she saw it, and she leaned over the fence, staring into its large, bright eyes and stroking its head compassionately. When it was time to go, her mother, sensing how much her daughter liked the animal, promised that they would return next year and visit the cow again. Nevertheless, Danielle worried that it would be lonely by itself, despite her mother's reassurance.

After a few more stops, the Avery family strolled contentedly along the farm's pathway and came upon a sign that read, 'Scarecrow Crossing Up Ahead.' They continued walking and after a few seconds, were in front of a large, well-crafted scarecrow. It was complete with a colorful straw hat, button eyes, overalls, and in its hands was a basket full of differently shaped buttons, including pumpkins, cats, witches, ghosts, crows, and bananas. Sean wondered out loud how whoever designed this area could have put ghosts and bananas together; they just didn't seem to fit.

The straw scarecrow had a wooden dowel coming up from its middle, giving it the appearance much like a popsicle on a stick. Behind it was another small barn and across from the scarecrow lay a few bushels of hay meant for sitting on.

The children's parents and Danielle sat down on the hay lumps to rest while the other kids went up to inspect the scarecrow. Suddenly they heard it utter *hello*. They laughed and waved to it, assuming that it was playing a taped greeting to acknowledge any passing pedestrians.

"Hello, scarecrow man," TJ piped up happily as he tugged on its overalls.

"Hello, little man," the scarecrow replied back. The children jumped.

"What's up?" Sean asked uncertainly.

"Nothing," the stiff scarecrow answered. Sean noted that its voice sounded deep and humanlike. A mischievous look crossed his face and, eager to learn the trick behind this scarecrow, he said, partly to himself, "He's probably programmed to recognize certain questions, so let's try a harder one. Hey, what's the capital of New Mexico?"

"Santa Fe," the scarecrow replied robotically.

"What's the opposite of cold?"

"Hot, of course."

"What's my favorite animal?"

"How would I know?"

Sean turned to Julia and said, "Ha! Well it's obvious they expanded his recorded messages a lot, but here's the real test."

He faced the scarecrow again, as Mandy circled it in thought and observation, and the children's parents smiled, knowing the trick.

"What color is my hair?"

"Brown," the scarecrow answered.

"Lucky guess, brown is a common color. What type of shirt am I wearing?"

The scarecrow was still. Sean beamed.

"Blue with a surfboard on the front," it replied a second later. The children were half-beginning to believe that they had discovered the world's first talking scarecrow.

"Little man," the scarecrow said. TJ jumped with joy at being personally addressed. "You may take a button from my collection if you wish," the scarecrow announced.

TJ practically knocked the talking scarecrow down in his excitement as he eagerly reached inside the basket and chose a pumpkin, happy that this time, the pumpkin choice was truly his.

Danielle got up and circled the scarecrow in surveillance, taking note of its hat, which had something that looked oddly similar to a small camera lens hidden in a crease.

"Scarecrow, will my cow be lonely?" she asked.

"No, that cow belongs to me. Don't worry, I'll take good care of her, especially for you. And you can come visit her any time you like."

The others were too busy thinking up new questions to ask the scarecrow to bother paying attention. But when Danielle looked through a window in the barn behind the scarecrow, she saw a man waving at her and she grinned.

Chapter 10

"I'm the little man," TJ screeched gleefully. Mandy chuckled and agreed, picked her little brother up, and swung him around.

Danielle and Sean were still talking about Pumpkin Acres, and how autumn would be here again soon. Sean suggested that we go back this year, like always.

It's strange how something that happened a year ago can seem to have occurred just yesterday. I can still smell the freshly-baked cookies at the farm's food store, and I still feel chilly when I remember walking outside on that cool day in late fall. I can still taste the salty air of the beach, and feel my father's firm hand, cupped around mine, as we ambled down the carnival street, or even when we took a walk around the neighborhood. Would these memories always seem so clear to us, or would we forget them little by little as our lives continued? I felt sure though, that the more we reminded ourselves of our past, the more real the memories would seem, and the closer our parents would be to us.

Why is it that certain things, like a lengthy school day or a trip to the dentist's office, seem to take forever at the time, but looking back on our entire lives with our parents seems to have only happened in a blink? And why did it seem as if now, that short period was up?

I stared at my siblings and wondered what the future held for us. Where would we be in ten years? In twenty? I was thankful that we had our grandparents to take care of us, but I again worried how TJ would feel, growing up without parents.

He'll be okay, I thought. No matter what, we would help him. We still had each other and that was one thing that was not going to change, I felt sure of it.

My thoughts still on my little brother, it was then that I looked up and scanned the room for TJ. My eyes found him in the corner of the gazebo, where he had originally found the jar. To my dismay, however, this time he was holding the container upside down, shaking it moderately hard and watching its contents roll on the floor.

Later, we would wonder what gave TJ the premonition that it was important to do what he was doing. Perhaps it was our parents telling him from inside his heart. Or, more likely, he had decided that it would be a fun, new game. But for whatever reason, TJ was now emptying the trinkets that we held so dear from the jar, on to the hard floor.

I yelped and scrambled over to him, clumsily falling flat on the floor just an inch away from his feet. The others came over and threw confused questions at him, but their voices became a buzz in the background. The world seemed to slow down to a leisurely pace as TJ bent his head close to mine and whispered, "It's my turn, Julia."

Then he then reached way down into the very bottom of the jar and pulled out the last object within it, the only one that had not plummeted out. I saw his fist closed tightly and then release as he dropped something shiny and pocket-sized into my open hand.

He gave a small toddler-shrug as he grinned, showing his teeth, and then began to scoop up the rocks and keepsakes that had fallen out of the jar.

The world returned back to its regular pace as Mandy, Sean, and Danielle bent down to help place the trinkets back into the jar. It was Danielle who first saw that I was staring curiously at an unfamiliar object in my hand.

She crouched down next to me to look as I sat up and crossed my legs. The others did the same a moment later.

"What is it, Jules?" Danielle asked quietly, as if I were holding something secret.

"I don't know," I replied truthfully.

The shiny object was a small computer disk, anyone could tell that from looking at it. But what was it doing here? Where did it come from?

None of us ever remembered putting it inside the memory jar, nor did we recall any particular memories that it might have been related with.

I examined its blank cover and then turned it over, still perplexed.

"What's on it?" Mandy inquired.

Sean smiled. "Well, there's only one way to find out."

Chapter 11

"*G*randma? Grandpa? Are you home?" I called out as we entered through the front door.

After searching the house, we discovered a note on the refrigerator saying that they were out running a few errands and would be back later. I began washing the dirty dishes in the sink, but my hands shook so much with apprehension, that I soon gave up and followed the others as they headed into the computer room.

Sean took a deep breath and put the disk into a small slot in the processor. The room was silent, except for TJ's untroubled humming, as we crowded around the screen, waiting for the disk to load. Mandy coughed and we all jumped, surprising ourselves with the extent of our anxiety.

Sean clicked on the 'Start' menu and selected the disk's icon cautiously, as if one wrong click might cause the room to detonate.

I am not sure what we had expected. I hardly imagine that we hoped it might be the missing link to the reason why our parents died, or a secret letter revealing to us the location of our parents when they fled the house during the fire. We did figure, however, that if whatever was contained on the small, unknown disk, was important enough to our parents to place it in our most special object, then it had to be significant to us as well.

Whatever we were expecting though, it was not this.

"It's a backup drive," Mandy declared as she read over the names of the folders that existed within the disk. There was a file labeled 'Backup Work Documents,' another titled 'Accounting Info,' one called 'Important Manuscript Copies,' and various other files.

"What's a backup drive for?" Danielle asked curiously.

"It keeps extra copies or files of important documents, just in case anything happens to the original ones," Sean replied, still staring at the screen. "I guess they put the disk in the memory jar for safekeeping."

I cannot say that we were totally disappointed, but we certainly did not think we could use any of the information the disk held, at least not at our ages. I could tell that its uselessness bothered us. We knew it belonged to our parents and therefore wanted it to be meaningful.

Sean continued to stroll down the long list and we examined the folder names intently, as if each one held a clue to a puzzle that just needed to be arranged. After a few minutes though, we gave up searching for something that was not there and Sean leaned back in his chair. His eyes were strained from squinting at the screen.

I saw TJ crawl into his lap and rock to and fro, probably wondering why we were suddenly sitting still. He then reached his small hands forward and sought the mouse, scrolling up and down rapidly a second later, laughing.

"Stop!" Sean screamed suddenly, but I noted that he sounded more eager than angry. He rolled the mouse slightly downward, back to a file he had seen when TJ was controlling the clicker, and Sean opened his mouth in awe.

At first I did not know what we were looking at. I did not understand why Sean's eyes were big or why Mandy had caught her breath and let out a small, *oh!* But after just a second, I spotted it too.

A file labeled 'Pictures.' It was a backup photo file.

The room was hushed for a moment that seemed to last an hour, but in truth, it was only an instant.

"Sean," Mandy practically shouted in his ear, "click on it! Click on the file!" But he ignored her and stayed still, his eyebrows furrowed and shoulders tense. Mandy reached hastily for the mouse to do it herself, but Sean snapped out of his stupor and beat her to it. He rested his hand on the mouse lightly and minimized the page.

I did not have much time to think in those few moments, but I could not understand why Sean was being so stubborn and unkind. But before I could get angry, Sean read my thoughts.

"It's not what you think, Julia. Look, I want to see the pictures as much as you guys do, but we should think this out for a minute first," he said, looking me straight in the eye.

"What is there to think about?" Mandy snapped in a huffy tone.

"Just hear me out, okay," he replied slowly, sounding as if he wanted to avoid a fight. "Now, listen. Anything can be in that file. For all we know, Mom and Dad saved hundreds of family pictures on there, and I'm not saying that's not a good thing. But the moment we open that file, the moment we click on that icon, everything is going to change."

"What's gonna change?" TJ said, patting Sean on the arm.

"You guys worked so hard to convince me, to convince each other, that the memories we shared mean everything in the world. Those pictures in there, they might be terrific, but will a snapshot really remind you of our parents and the good times we had with them? No, it will be something pretty to look at. I'm not saying that they won't make us feel better, but after a while, I'm sure we'll forget about the little details that are in fact so special, and only see an image of the photo when we think about the beach, or the carnival, or even just spending time together at home," Sean was on his feet now, his voice loud and sure.

"Pictures can be wonderful, but our parents would have put together a photo album, instead of a memory jar, if they wanted us to reminisce with pictures, but they didn't. We didn't. We have the memory jar, and it triggers the memories in our minds, and as we talk about them and remember, they become real. Even more real then a photograph, because the living and breathing people who were involved with them are right here. I've been thinking about this a lot. The jar is so important, I now see that and I wish you would too. All along, it was meant to help us remember, yes, but also to bring us together. Can't you see? All along it has been more than just a glass jar. It has been our own treasure-trove.

"If we open the file without thinking and just act, then we might forget about our treasure, we might put the jar away and never take it out again. It may disappear just like our parents. And we can't let that happen. We just can't. We cannot forget like I tried so hard to do, but we also cannot live in the past. We have to get on with our lives, but still remember, so in our hearts our parents will never really be gone.

"And what if there aren't any pictures in there? What if Mom and Dad never got a chance to download any? We can't just give up then. We can't just go back to not living.

"I am thankful that we may have found pictures, but they are not some second option to the jar that will replace it. We didn't do all that retelling, and pour all of our hearts into the stories for nothing, did we? Did we share them just so we could merely put them aside and move on? Right from the start, we wanted pictures of our parents, of our previous lives, but the memories have been *enough* all along. They have brought us together and helped remind us

that stories from our past don't just fade away, they live on."
Sean paused as if to let it settle in, but I could tell he was
taking the breath that he had been holding in for so long.

I was stunned. I had never seen my brother feel so
strongly about something before, and for a moment, I
closed my eyes. And I realized he was right. *Yes.*

"Yes. Yes!" I shouted, jumping up and running into his
open arms. I knew he finally understood, and I realized that
I myself hadn't really understood until this very minute.
Mandy and Danielle got up and hugged us too, while TJ sat
on the floor in the center, his arms around Sean's leg. We
stood there together for a long time, until Mandy broke the
silence.

"You're right Sean. We won't forget about our treasure-trove. Never. It's the most important thing," Mandy
whispered, wiping her eyes.

Sean laughed quietly, probably for no particular reason other than because it was better than crying. "Okay,
good then, as long as we remember that before we open the
file."

We positioned ourselves back around the computer
slowly, gathering around Sean in the chair. This time I was
not nervous. If there were family pictures in there, then we
would be grateful and overjoyed, but if not, then at least we
would always have each other, and the memories in our
hearts.

Sean took another deep breath. "No matter what happens, we're still a family." Mandy and I nodded and all eyes
were on the screen as he reopened the page, pointed the
mouse on the folder, pressed down, and clicked...

Chapter 12

❧

*T*he sun shone high above the clouds, illuminating the sky to the point where it looked magical. Mandy and I held hands as we walked in front, glancing back every few minutes to check on the others. We watched as a lone squirrel skidded toward us, and then scurried away as if we were a potential threat. I heard TJ laugh and point as it ran up a large tree, Spiderman-style.

A cloud drifted over the bright sun, shading the earth for us, and we were pleased to have a cool break on this searing morning. We were striding along a familiar path on the sidewalk, a path that held memories tucked in its footway cracks, dirt edges, and even beneath the fresh grass sprouting on the sides. I heard Mandy sigh quietly beside me and I wondered if it was out of contentment, or anxiety.

We neared the perfect mailbox and continued through the once-stunning front lawn without pausing. I was happy to see that the land looked a bit greener and fuller physically, though still empty in a way only we understood.

We went directly to the pearly white gazebo and sat down on one of the long, cushioned benches together. It had been three weeks since we had last visited and found the small disk, and I thought about how much we had changed. We had all taken what Sean reminded us of to heart; we were living again.

In just a short period of time, we had revisited Sandy Pleasure Beach with our grandparents, taken a hike and a camping trip, and had numerous picnic lunches (it had become something of a tradition). And I was back to reading my mystery novels every night. But more than that, we had started truly acting like a family again, amongst ourselves and with our grandparents, who now created new memories with us.

Lost in my thoughts, I did not see the tiny, yellow bird that had flown up until it landed beside me on the bench, its head cocked to the left. I smiled and watched it, until TJ came up in what he thought was a quiet manner but really was not, and the beautiful bird flew off, tweeting in a way that sounded more like laughter. Laughter had become contagious for me these days, even the twittering of a bird was amusing, I suppose, because I was soon smiling and chuckling.

I took everything in as I gazed poignantly at my surroundings, knowing without even looking at my brothers and sisters, that they were doing the same.

Sean got up and took TJ by the hand, leading him over to a part of the interior white wood that he had noticed had a crack. He lifted TJ up and together they pulled until the crack widened, leaving a small piece of white wood lying in the palm of the young boy's hand. This was not a surprise to Mandy, Danielle, or me.

We watched silently as Sean directed TJ over to the jar which we had brought along with us, and which was now resting on a bench. TJ had the honor of dropping the white wood softly inside. Sean closed the lid tightly.

We had decided that since we had taken the disk out, it was our obligation to put something special back in its place. But even more, we had decided that this whole adventure, the good and the bad, had become a memory in itself, one that we would retell in the future to our children and grandchildren, and to each other.

Visiting the gazebo this time was not on impulse; we had spent many nights discussing what to do and we had come to this conclusion when we were sure it was for the best, for everyone.

There was only one reason that we had returned to the gazebo, and that was to say goodbye.

Memories are so essential to a person's life. The mistakes made in the past and remembered help confirm that they will not happen again, memories remind people about different times that may have disappeared, they give a clear picture of loved ones that are lost, and they help people decide what they want to do with the rest of their lives. We learned that memories are precious. They are sacred.

But the past cannot dictate our lives.

Our parents would have wanted us to live, to be happy, to prosper. And to do this, we cannot dwell in the past, or on the past. We must move on. That does not mean, however, that we will ever forget about our past lives, our previous house, or our parents. When we need them, they will be there, in our memories, and when even they cannot soothe the pain, then we will always have each other.

If there is one thing that we have learned, it is that memories are a part of us, and forever will be, as we continue on with our lives.

Mandy took out a square object from the blue knapsack that she brought and leaned it carefully on the floor against the gazebo's wall. We stared at the frame, and then back at each other for a moment, before Sean picked TJ up, Mandy took Danielle by the hand, and we prepared to depart. As we left, we each touched the sturdy, white walls lightly with our fingertips, knowing that this would probably be the last time we would return.

As we walked away, I turned back for one last glance. Though we were some distance away, I could still vaguely make out the picture in the frame that was leaning against one of the walls. It was one of the many pictures we had now, all of them acquired from the disk. A tall, handsome man stood next to his lovely wife, their hands placed lovingly on the shoulders of their five children.

And they were smiling. Smiling at the world, smiling at the gazebo, smiling at the memory jar which would always be cherished. And I knew that they were smiling at us.

Part 3

The Unexpected Trinket

Chapter 13

3 Months Later

*T*he familiar hum of excited chatter and the clatter of lockers being opened and slammed shut reached my ears, the usual end-of-day melody. I knelt and sorted through my locker, picking out the books and folders I would need to take home for the night. My first year of middle school taught me many things, one of them being nimbleness of fingers. If you weren't quick at your locker, the possibility of getting tripped over, banged up, or, of course, missing your bus was more than high. I could speak from experience.

Still on my knees, I reached upward and fumbled around in the top compartment. I quickly felt for my lunch container and attempted to drag it down into my bag. It slipped from my fingers and landed on my head. I promised myself that by next year, at least, I would be able to endure a school day without getting bruised up, and reached back upward again for my umbrella.

It had been raining so hard that morning that it had sounded as if drums were beating in my ears as it poured on my umbrella. At the bus stop, Mandy, Sean, and I had each had protection, but still somehow managed to get soaking wet from head to foot. Our bus driver had seemed particular grumpy as we treaded mud and slush through the aisle.

Our hair was plastered to our faces, dripping huge droplets onto the floor.

I silently prayed that it had quieted down outside. I dreaded another ride on our humid bus, full of kids throwing candy wrappers across the seats and people complaining out loud when you asked if you could sit with them. It was safe to say that bus rides were not my favorite part of the school day.

While I groped around for my green umbrella, I felt something smooth and papery. I stood up and pulled the note from my locker, unfolding it. I recognized Sean's handwriting immediately:

Don't forget about our plans for after school today. I don't want to be left alone in the rain! Meet me by the front door. See you later!

-S

I let out a squeak, realizing with a little embarrassment that I *had* forgotten. I hoped I hadn't kept him waiting too long as I stuffed the last of my things into my backpack, crumpled the note up and shoved it into my pocket, and slammed the door shut a little too hard. I was already racing toward the front of the building as the locker's loud echo vibrated off the gradually emptying hallway. I couldn't help but feel thankful that I wouldn't have to endure another bus ride today.

I managed to shove open the school's front door while opening my umbrella and soon found myself once again in the pouring rain.

"Took you long enough," I heard Sean chuckle through the drone of rainfall, his face hidden beneath his own umbrella. "You forgot, didn't you?"

"No, I didn't forget," I said, smiling. We both knew how badly I was at lying.

"Well, come on. I'm sure Grandpa's already waiting," he responded, before glancing in both directions and heading across the school's parking lot. I followed close behind and watched as the trail of buses off to the right side of the building began to make their way toward the students' homes. I waved to one as it passed by in front of us.

"Did you have a good day at school today?" Sean said conversationally.

"Pretty good," I said, "My science teacher said we are going to start our dissecting section soon though." I shuddered. "With my luck, we'll probably dissect something really gross, like a frog."

"Don't be silly," Sean said, "You won't dissect a frog." I sighed with relief. "That's not until next year," he added. I cringed.

We continued on, reaching the other side of the parking lot, and turned right onto the sidewalk surrounding our school.

I saw Sean reach into his backpack and draw out a small flash drive, cupping it securely in his hand. We had decided the day before to make a copy of the pictures we had gotten from the disk in the memory jar. We planned to put it in the bank for safekeeping. We knew from experience that you could never be too cautious. What you had one day was not always guaranteed to be there the next.

Sean and I had volunteered to drop it off at the bank with our grandfather, and I was eager to reach our destination and get out of the rain. Rainstorms had a different meaning for me these days. I knew the power that they contained.

After walking for just a few minutes, I was able to spot the building, located just down the block from school. It was relatively new, very large, and extremely luxurious-looking. I always thought it almost seemed too grand to be a bank; a palace or a hotel seemed a more appropriate fit.

I noticed our grandparents' car as we ran up the great steps and through the humongous double doors. Our grandfather was waiting for us just inside, holding TJ by the hand. Together we walked into the main room of the bank.

As Grandpa went to talk to one of the bank's tellers, Sean, TJ, and I took a seat in the comfy chairs lining the back wall. I saw Sean grab a chocolate chip cookie from a tray on a small coffee table and lean back, relaxed. TJ grabbed three. I gazed up at the beautifully-painted high ceiling, lost in a daydream. I only snapped out of my reverie when Sean tugged at my shoulder, pointing at our grandfather who was signaling for us to follow.

We shuffled to the opposite side of the bank. The teller was in the lead. She was a cheerful young woman with blond hair that was so light it looked white. I remembered coming here with my mother one time when she dropped off some papers for safekeeping. That is why I wasn't surprised when the woman ushered us through a large door that led into a room filled from the floor up with wall boxes. TJ, on the other hand, seemed to be absolutely amazed at this phenomenon. His little jaw dropped open and he pointed up and down, to each side, and behind him in little-kid awe. Sean and I couldn't help but laugh.

Grandpa produced a long key from his pocket and handed it to Sean. I noticed the banker had a key in her hand as well and I remembered that both keys were needed to retrieve the box, as an extra safety precaution. Sean then gave her our key and she used them both. After she opened the square door she pulled out a long thin metal box. Our safe deposit box.

The woman smiled as she handed the box to Sean, before gesturing toward yet another door. This led to a separate room where people could place their possessions in their boxes in private. Sean and I entered by ourselves, our grandfather and TJ lingering behind with the woman.

Inside the 'privacy room' was a small table with a few chairs surrounding it. The room was darker than the main safe and I waited for my eyes to adjust. I then took a seat while Sean placed the box on top of the cold, stone surface of the table. He lifted the lid and together we bent over to look inside. A few documents rested in envelopes on the bottom, most likely birth certificates, but otherwise it was mostly empty.

Sean lightly dropped the flash drive containing many of our family pictures into the box. I surprised myself by immediately feeling light and happy. I guess I hadn't realized just how anxious I was to make sure our photographs would always be secure.

I bounced off my chair and began to skip to the door when I noticed that Sean wasn't behind me. He was still bent over at the table, his face scrunched up as if he were concentrating on something.

"What is it?" I asked, curious, as I went back over to him.

"Hey, take a look at this and tell me if you think it sounds familiar," he responded, pulling a slip of paper out from inside the box. It was old and a little crumpled up, as if it had been written on and used a lot. I spread it out on the table and understood almost instantly what Sean meant. I nodded at him.

"Thought so," he said. He folded the piece of paper up and put it inside his jean's pocket. Then he got up and followed me out the door. We squinted in the bright light of the safety deposit boxes room.

"There they are," our grandfather said cheerily. "All ready to go?"

"All ready," I replied. As we headed back to the main section of the bank and then out to the car, I couldn't help but think about the paper inside Sean's pocket. The paper our parents had obviously touched and written on numerous times.

It was absolutely unmistakable, at least, for anyone in our immediate family. The sheet of paper contained merely a list of words, words that may have seemed placed together randomly. However, Sean and I understood what they meant.

It was a list of objects that were very important to us. Our memory jar trinkets.

Chapter 14

"*H*mm, you're right of course," I heard Mandy say. I was at my father's old desk, finishing up my math homework. I was in an oddly good mood. It probably had to do with the fact that I actually wasn't struggling with my math work tonight. Math was never one of my best subjects and we were working on fractions now, but strangely they seemed to come quite easily to me. I wondered why I always had trouble with the simple things in math, but when my teacher warned us that it might get tricky, I had no problems. I decided to accept my strange malfunction without complaint.

I had a feeling, however, that my good mood could also be attributed to the fact that I was working on my schoolwork in the same room, at the same desk even, that my father once worked at when he was a kid. It made me feel closer to him somehow.

It was late, and Sean and Danielle had joined Mandy and I a few minutes before. Our father's old room had changed since the summer, yet it was still the same. Our grandparents had replaced the single bed and ancient couch with two smaller beds. They had also added another desk, Mandy's. But the walls were untouched, the closet not cleared out, and the window drapes left alone. I didn't want to alter anything major, instead preserving the room our dad had lived in just the way he had lived in it.

"But...why?" Sean responded, bringing me back to their discussion. Sean had just shown Mandy and Danielle the paper he had taken from the bank, the list of our treasure-trove keepsakes.

She shrugged. "I guess Mom and Dad knew how important memories were to our family and wanted to make sure we kept track of them."

I noticed Danielle hadn't said anything for a while and glanced around to see what she was doing. I saw her sitting on Mandy's bed with the memory jar in her lap, sifting through its contents.

Mandy stood up and stretched.

"Well, I don't know how to say this nicely, but can you leave Sean? I'm really tired and I want to get to bed on time." Sean made a face of mock offense.

"Are you almost done, Jules?" she asked me, rolling her eyes at our brother.

"Yeah, perfect timing," I said as I began to pack up my work.

Mandy picked up the list and looked over it again, still standing. She smiled.

"Mom and Dad did a good job of keeping track of them. All...," she went silent for a moment, counting, "fifteen of them."

"Fourteen," Danielle said. I turned around and saw that she still had the memory jar in her hands.

"What?" Mandy replied, surprised.

"Fourteen. There are fourteen trinkets in the jar. I just counted."

Mandy looked over the list again. Then she looked up.

"There's fifteen by their count," she said.

"That's strange," I murmured.

Sean, Danielle, and I got up and crowded around Mandy, who still clutched the list. Though it was getting later by the minute, curiosity had taken hold of us. One by one, we sorted through the objects listed on the piece of paper, making sure that we had them. The farther down the list we went, the more worried I became. What if we had lost one? Where could it possibly have gone?

"The pearl," Mandy read.

"Check," Danielle responded, pulling the pink pearl from the jar.

Mandy continued to read off the names of our memory jar objects and I gave a small sigh of relief each time we were reassured that one wasn't missing.

A little over halfway down the list, glancing over Mandy's shoulder, I became suddenly confused at the next trinket. She was in her concentration mode, however, and didn't seem to notice.

"RR," she said.

"What?" Sean asked loudly.

"RR," she said again, this time unsurely.

We looked around at each other.

"RR," Sean said, "What in the world is 'RR'?"

"I don't know," Mandy replied, squinting at the paper.

"Well, let's come back to it," I suggested. "Maybe it will come to us." But as we continued on with the list, and discovered that all of the other trinkets were accounted for, there was no denying that 'RR' was the object we had been looking for. The fifteenth trinket. And we had no idea what it was.

We decided to look at it from a logical point of view. If there were fourteen trinkets in the jar, and those fourteen objects were matched to fourteen names on the paper, then to discover the location of the fifteenth name on the list, the unknown one, we had to figure out what in fact it was we were looking for. In the beginning, we picked our brains in an orderly manner, scanning our memories carefully, and tried to put ourselves in our parents' shoes. After forty-five minutes of hard thinking with no success, we were forced to resort to a less organized approach to our reasoning.

"How about...'Roving Rabbit'?" Sean said, not bothering to hide the boredom in his voice.

"Sean, that's almost as bad as your 'Red Railroad' or 'Ranting Rhino'," Mandy replied in an equally monotonous tone.

"Well, I don't see you coming up with anything better," was his response. He stifled a yawn.

"RR, RR," I muttered. Perhaps if I said the strange acronym enough my mind could transform it into something decipherable.

"Maybe it doesn't stand for something. Maybe that's just its name," Mandy suggested.

"Who knows," I said, "but I think I give up. For tonight at least. We can think about it some more tomorrow." It was really late now and my curiosity had dampened a long time ago. Sean expressed similar feelings.

"Yeah, you're right," he said, "Besides, if there aren't any other trinkets in the jar, and we don't remember losing, or even seeing for that matter, any acronym-RR-mystery-type thing, then what could it really be?"

"Well, I don't give up," Mandy said in her usual determined tone, "Mom and Dad wrote it down, and I'm sure it means something." Sean rolled his eyes at me.

"Okay, well if you figure out anything, let me know. Good night." He padded out of the room. Danielle had left for hers a half-hour before, so it was just Mandy and me. I quickly got changed for bed and left to brush my teeth. When I came back, I found Mandy, fully dressed, fast asleep on my bed. I debated waking her up, but she looked so tired, so instead I crawled under her covers and was asleep as well within seconds.

Chapter 15

I glanced at the clock and shifted the weight of my backpack onto the floor when I realized that we still had a little while until we had to leave. I was glad to be able to prolong my stay at home, even for just a few minutes, thus delaying the upcoming Thursday school day. We were sitting around the kitchen table, all five of us, finishing up a breakfast of toast and jelly, eggs, and OJ, while our grandmother busied herself near the sink.

When I had woken up earlier, a new dedication to discovering the mystery behind 'RR' had overtaken me, surprising Mandy greatly. As we had gotten ready, we had brainstormed some more, though with no success. We just could not remember anything connected with us that fit the strange acronym.

At the breakfast table, I was even more surprised than Mandy had been to find that Sean shared the same newly-discovered enthusiasm.

"Grandma, do you have any idea what 'RR' might mean? To our parents?" he asked. I had little hope that she would recognize it, so her answer was unexpected.

"You know, it sounds familiar. I can't quite put my finger on it though," she replied slowly, placing her hands on her hips.

"Really?" Sean said. At that moment, our grandfather entered the room, a newspaper in his hands. He answered for his wife.

"Yes. That does sound vaguely familiar. RR. Hmm…well it seems we're having a senior moment, children," Grandpa said.

"That does sometimes happen when you're seniors," Grandma added with a laugh.

"Come on you guys, we'd better go," Mandy said, "It's getting late and the bus will be here soon."

We grabbed our bags, said good-bye to Danielle, TJ, and our grandparents, and rushed out the door. At the bus stop, we greeted our new friend Lucas, a small, dark-haired boy in Mandy's grade who lived in our grandparents' neighborhood.

"School time," I said with a sigh. I wasn't really in the mood for seven consecutive hours of classes.

"Yeah, I know," Lucas replied, "but, hey, at least there's only one more day to go, right?"

"Oh, yeah, I almost forgot!" I yelled loudly. Because of a 'teachers in-service day,' a wonderful gift had been bestowed upon us, something students across the country hope for and dream about: a four-day week. I finally had some incentive to get me through the day.

Between paying attention to my studies and reminding myself that this was the last day of the week, my mind continued to drift back toward the infamous 'RR.' I began to see the letter R everywhere; I had never known it was so abundant in my everyday life. Yet I still could not figure it out. But though my frustration grew, I could not deny the nagging sense that those two, unfamiliar letters were important. Very important. Maybe it was just due to the fact that my parents had written it down, had traced those elegant two letters with a pencil. I decided that any mystery connected with Mom and Dad was worth solving.

And with that in mind, I continued to think.

The day passed by without much event, but not quite as slowly as I had dreaded it might. Most of my teachers sensed the air of excitement amongst their students about the upcoming long weekend. In order not to stifle any weekend plans, we were given easy classes with little homework.

Despite the fact that I hadn't thought of any particularly hopeful R-words, by the end of the day my spirits were high. I only had about an hour of schoolwork to do before Monday, and I was on the brink of a three-day weekend. Though I loved middle school so much more than elementary school—the freedom, the multiple teachers, being in a school without six-year-olds, cute as they were—I was more than ready for a little break.

At 3:00, I could once again be found kneeling by my locker, a sense of déjà vu surrounding me. I waved goodbye to my friends, slammed my locker shut, and ran out to the bus. I took a seat next to Mandy and saw Sean sitting with Lucas behind us. They were deeply involved in a heated discussion concerning video games, a topic that I am not afraid to admit eludes me.

Mandy and I exchanged the pitiful R-ideas we had each come up with, sighed together, and waited for the bus to reach our grandparents' neighborhood.

Our luck changed when we reached the house, however. After I hung up the light jacket I had taken to school, I followed Mandy and Sean into the kitchen for our usual afternoon snack. Danielle was still at her school, due to be home in about thirty minutes, and we found TJ sitting at the table, eating from a bowl filled with gummy bears.

"Perfect," Sean said, grabbing a handful before TJ could block his attempt. TJ began to protest, but was quickly distracted by the remaining fifty gummies.

"Did Grandma and Grandpa really say you could have all those before dinner?" I asked him.

"Yes!" he cried, nodding his head excitedly. Despite his cuteness, I seriously doubted it.

"Just great, you know how he gets when he has sugar. This is not going to be pretty," Mandy said, sounding stern, but with the hint of a smile on her lips.

As if that were the cue he was waiting for, TJ then jumped up off the chair he was sitting on, literally leaping into the air, and landed on the tile floor with a loud 'smack' before sprinting out the door.

We looked at each other. Sean raised an eyebrow. We could hear screaming throughout the house and the pitter-patter of bare feet on carpeting. Then, as if this was part of his everyday routine, TJ ran back into the kitchen, climbed onto the chair, and continued his sugary snacking.

We hadn't moved a muscle.

"Well, that was quite a show," Grandma said, entering the kitchen, laughing. I loved my grandmother's laugh. It was high-pitched and had an irresistible tinkling edge to it that made it almost impossible not to join in.

She took the bowl away from TJ and replaced it with a bag of pretzels, which he accepted happily.

"I guess I'll have to remember to hide the gummies from now on."

We each grabbed a handful of the pretzels. I was on my way up to our room when something my grandmother said stopped me. Suddenly, after all those hours of devising possibilities, with two simple words, the mystery was solved. Or at least, a part of it.

"You guys, I almost forgot to tell you. I've been think-ing all day about what you asked me this morning. Of course, it came to me the moment I picked up one of the books on our coffee table. RR– The Reading Retreat."

The room went silent and I processed the two words in my mind, noting their unfamiliarity. I was taken aback; I had expected the answer to be at least somewhat recogniz-able. We had assumed it was in fact guessable after all.

"The Reading...what?" Sean asked, surprise in his voice.

"The Reading Retreat," my grandmother said carefully, seeming to sense that her words held more meaning than she had reckoned for. "Where did you kids hear about that anyway?"

"Just when we were going through some of Mom and Dad's old things," Sean said hastily, eager to get back on the subject. "What's the Reading Retreat?"

"Oh, it is b-e-e-e-eautiful! You guys would absolutely love it there. You know, I'm surprised your parents never took you up to see it. Guess they never got a chance, it is quite far away," she said.

"But, what *is* it?" Sean pressed.

She took in our confused expressions and explained. According to her, it was the most extraordinary bookstore in the world, all the way out in Washington. Our father had designed it. In fact, it was his first major architectural project.

"He used to call it 'RR' for short," she added with a light laugh, her mind far away. "It really is something special."

"The Reading Retreat. A bookstore. That our dad designed," I said slowly. Then I looked around. We were all thinking the same thing: what could that possibly have to do with the memory jar?

We told our grandmother that we would be upstairs, and she said she'd call us down as soon as dinner was ready. Then we rushed up the steps together. Except for TJ of course, who was still munching on his pretzels.

As soon as we reached Mandy's and my room, I closed the door and we lounged about on the bed and at the desks.

"Are we missing something?" Mandy asked, "I mean, I'm assuming that the bookstore *isn't* trinket-sized."

"Not to mention the fact that we don't remember actually losing anything from the jar," I muttered. "This doesn't make sense." I turned to my brother to get some feedback.

"Hmm..." was all I got as a response.

"How can a bookstore, that Dad designed, but we've never even been to, be the missing memory jar keepsake?" I prompted, keeping my eyes on him.

He was silent for a minute. Then he jumped up.

"Hey wait a sec. Maybe we are looking at this the wrong way. Grandma said that the Reading Retreat was in *Washington*, right?"

"Yes," Mandy and I said together slowly, not following.

"Well...can you think of anything else special that happened in Washington?"

I stared at him, confused. I was about to utter 'no,' when suddenly an unexpected memory trickled into my brain. I could see my father coming home after a long trip away for work, bringing home a present to his eager children...

"Dad got the memory jar in Washington," Mandy said, echoing my thoughts.

"Exactly!" Sean said excitedly.

"But wait," I cut in, "what does that *mean*? That the *memory jar* is the last trinket?"

"Yes! That must be it. It makes sense. And anyway what else could it be?"

I still wasn't convinced. Neither was Mandy.

"Sean," she yelled loudly to get his attention, for he was jumping around, confident in his guess, "why would they write 'Reading Retreat' on the list then?"

"Who knows?" he replied, "Maybe they sold the jars at the RR, or near it, or something." His tone was dismissive and I could tell from his voice that the mystery was solved to him.

"Well, I guess it will have to do," Mandy said, referring to his explanation.

We put the topic aside and excitedly discussed the long weekend ahead of us. Danielle soon joined us and we only spent a few brief moments filling her in on what Grandma had revealed. No one had too much homework to get done and we talked about some fun things we could do together. After a little while, our grandmother called us downstairs for dinner.

The others rushed out and I followed behind, my hand lingering on the light switch. Instead of turning it off straightaway, I turned around and looked at the memory jar, resting on top of Mandy's desk.

It did make sense, I decided. I could see Mom and Dad considering the special jar just as important as the other trinkets within it.

I guess it will have to do, I thought, repeating Mandy's words. We could never know for sure, after all.

I flipped down the switch and the room darkened.

Chapter 16

"**S**urprise!"

My grandmother held up a bunch of plane tickets that were in her hands. Before I had a chance to react, to wonder where we were going or why we were going there, the answers to my questions burst out of her. I could tell that she was excited and I hadn't seen her this happy in a long time. I let the smile that wanted to form appear around my lips.

"We're going to Washington! To visit the Reading Retreat!"

Suddenly it made sense. Grandma had been beaming uncontrollably since breakfast, even humming and singing while we ate. I should have known she had a secret bubbling up within her.

"Really?" Mandy yelled, "We're flying to Washington?" Our grandmother nodded and we all jumped up and down excitedly. We didn't care that we looked like little kids. Who doesn't love vacations? Especially last-minute ones.

"You guys have been so good lately and we figured you needed a break. They have some nice cities and places to visit in that area. This will be a pleasant way to spend your long weekend. Besides, we think your parents would have wanted you to see the Reading Retreat at some point," Grandfather chimed in.

"Yes, you children mentioning yesterday how you've never been there got me thinking. *I'd* really love to see it again. And I know you'll love it there too."

I smiled at her, but couldn't help but wonder how much time they planned to have us spend at the RR. Though I loved books and books and books, there was only so much you could do in a bookstore. How different could this one really be? I decided that, nevertheless, it would be nice to see something our father designed.

We rushed up the stairs and started packing—our flight was scheduled to take off in just a few hours. Grandma and Grandpa told us to pack a day's and a night's worth of clothing, because they planned to have us stay at a hotel in Seattle. Luckily, our grandparents had some old luggage lying around, which we used.

Somehow, the seven of us managed to be down the stairs, luggage in hand, and ready to go in just a single hour. Mandy had helped TJ pack. It was hard not to smile when he marched down the steps, a small, neon green luggage in his grip, our dad's old one from his childhood, and a baseball cap on his head.

We were doing great with time as we rushed out the door and soon enough we turned onto the highway. We probably would have made it to the airport with more than enough time to spare, too, if TJ hadn't drank three full glasses of milk for breakfast. It would have also helped if we had remembered to shut the garage door before we left, not the moment we got back onto the freeway.

When at last we pulled into the large airport parking lot, we ran inside with our luggage trailing behind us loudly. The common phrase 'arrived in the nick of time' flashed repeatedly in my mind. Everything was a big blur until we exited the terminal, our things safely stowed away, and we entered the plane. The moment we sat down in the big, comfy chairs, I finally felt like I could breathe again. I relaxed, looking out the window. As we took off, I continued to stare out the glass and watched everything get smaller and smaller as we rose higher and higher into the air.

I heard Danielle next to me and Sean up front talking soothingly to TJ, who has never been the biggest fan of flying. And then tiredness overcame me and I couldn't help but notice how the fluffy clouds looked so much like pillows. My eyelids grew droopy and my vision dimmed...

"This street definitely looks familiar! I'm positive this time," Grandfather said.

Because this was the eighth time I'd heard that in the last forty-five minutes, I didn't even bother getting my hopes up. Although my feet felt slightly sore from all the walking we had been doing, I was glad at least that we didn't have to lug around our luggage anymore. We had dropped it off at the hotel and it felt great to be able to walk freely at last.

I suddenly heard Mandy gasp beside me and I looked up at her quickly to see what the matter was. She was staring straight ahead of her, an awed look on her face. I followed her gaze.

In front of us was easily the most beautiful building I had ever seen in my life. Almost entirely white, it was comprised of exactly the right combination of smooth edges and raised tower-like structures to give it the vague impression of a castle. Large stained-glass windows occupied the frontal areas on each side of the wide double doors. The colors that made up the windows were so vivid from the sunlight and so fantastic that it was hard to tear your eyes from them. A long, curving pathway led up to the entrance and elegant rocking chairs lined the front porch, cushioned with pillows of a variety of shades of blue. The path was edged with a rainbow of pretty glass stones.

On each side of the pathway leading up to the building was a multitude of tall trees. It looked as though they intentionally grew so that their leaves arched together, forming a canopy above. Because of the season, their fall leaves shown with brilliant colors that merged nicely against the glass windows.

A large fountain, made up entirely of white stone, was placed in the center of the front lawn. It was shaped like an enormous, open book, with pages nearly as long as I was tall. In the middle of the fountain, surrounding the book on all sides, were little stone children clutching at the novel, obviously enchanted by the story.

The beautiful setting seemed to hold one's attention entirely. I felt momentarily filled with sadness at the thought of walking past it, but then I noticed the words emblazoned above the building entrance. I then saw our grandparents gesture for us to follow them through the awning of maple trees.

"*This* is the Reading Retreat?" Sean asked, unbelievingly.

"Amazing, isn't it?" Grandma replied with tears in her eyes.

I understood Sean's bewilderment. I knew that I at least hadn't had any clue how incredible the RR would be. It was just a bookstore after all, right?

Wrong.

The moment we stepped inside, entering the grand front entrance room, we could instantly tell how incorrect our simple expectations had been.

The first thing that caught my attention was the huge bookshelves towering over us, row after row after row of them. This was probably the only feature that resembled other bookstores, however. Every inch of the high walls was decorated. They either had swirls of fantastic color or beautiful paintings of the covers of famous novels.

The room had a homey feeling to it, despite its vast size. Cozy armchairs and loveseats were scattered throughout, and lovely sculptures could be found at almost every turn.

As we walked down the main aisle and our view opened up farther, we soon discovered that the store's delight didn't end there.

Passageways caught our eyes, leading into entirely separate rooms or areas filled with even more books and surprises.

There was a large teen section, with all the latest young adult novels, brown and aqua bean bag chairs, and its own small café. Mandy got so caught up in this area that it was hard to pull her away and continue on.

The children's section was beyond words. Giving the impression of a large tree house, it was slightly raised above the floor. A small set of stairs could be taken to reach its wooden ground and it was surrounded by realistic-looking leaves and branches. The inside was brightly colored and a large children's play structure occupied the back, with young kids climbing up and down its many levels. The top level had large telescopes that could be looked through to see the entire store. The tree house's floor had many tables in the shape of small tree trunks with an excess of colorful paper, crayons for drawing, and board books for toddlers.

There were other incredible rooms such as the 'Fairy Fireside' that was an inviting circular space. It was complete with a handsome fireplace surrounded by an abundance of chairs and quilts. The fireplace had beautiful carvings of fairies around it and gorgeous sketches of magical creatures occupied the round walls.

The 'Orchid Oasis' was entirely decorated with orchids of every variety and the flowery fragrance that enveloped the room was both magnificent and soothing.

The beauty that incorporated such rooms was overpowering.

The bookstore's main café had many types of coffees, teas, and baked goods. The ornate, wooden tables around the snack bar had a complimentary list of the latest bestsellers to look over, as well as dishes of small candies.

I noticed the same colorful glass stones that had lined the sidewalk around the building too. They were built into pretty, swirling designs in the bookshelves, and could also be spotted around the entrances of the intriguing rooms and other various places as well. I thought they added a nice touch to the setting.

As we walked around, no one said very much. We seemed to be too busy gaping and pointing and gasping. When we had circled the bookstore, looking over everything at least once, if only briefly, we finally seemed to be able to move our mouths again.

"Dad designed this?" Sean asked in a small voice, an awed expression on his face.

I was momentarily startled as I realized that I had forgotten for a minute why in particular this incredible place was meaningful to us.

Our grandparents nodded together, smiling, and told us that we could stay as long as we wanted. Then we all scattered in different directions.

Now that I could fully grasp the fact that our father had been such a big part of this bookstore, it had a different meaning to me. As I ran my hand along the shiny bookshelves, I wondered if he touched the same wood so many years ago. When I gazed up at the high, dark ceiling, with stars and planets painted delicately on it, I wondered if he too had watched it and felt at peace. I knew I did now.

It was hard not to feel close to my parents when I walked around the building, admiring its beauty, its family friendliness, and its creativity. I heard laughter almost everywhere I went, and I understood; it was hard not to smile in this place.

After a while, I wound up in the mystery section. This didn't surprise me. It was a dark room on the far right side of the building with a huge, incredible magnifying glass built into the wall above its entrance. I smiled as I stepped inside. My fingers lightly traced the edges of the novels as I walked around.

Wanting a souvenir of the incredible bookstore to take with me, I decided to buy one of the books. I browsed around to find something that looked interesting. Soon, I spotted one that included a haunted house, mysterious clues, and a suspicious neighbor. Perfect.

I walked to the checkout counter and encountered an elderly woman with a friendly expression on her face. I purchased the novel and thanked her. I immediately began to turn away when she suddenly stopped me.

"You must be a first timer here," she said warmly. I nodded, confused. She then reached behind the counter and pulled out a bookmark, handing it to me.

"We always hand out complimentary bookmarks to our customers when they purchase books," she explained, "It's a tradition we've kept since the Reading Retreat's opening. One of its architects suggested it."

I smiled and thanked her again. I sat down in one of the many armchairs and stared at the bookmark in my hand. It, like everything else in the bookstore, was beautiful, and I looked forward to using it since it clearly surpassed all of my other bookmarks.

I recognized the designs on it as being similar to the ones on the bookshelves: wonderful swirls of color, abstract, but lovely. Those same colorful stones were there again, nicely woven into the pattern.

My mouth suddenly gaped open. I brought the bookmark closer to my face and stared hard at the small stones making up the design. I knew them from somewhere and it took me just an instant to figure it out. I left the chair and found Mandy and Danielle in the Orchid Oasis. I showed them what I had discovered. Then together, we sought out Sean and TJ and filled them in.

Looking back on it, it seemed so obvious. We should have been able to tell from the moment we walked up the pathway; our wonder at the magnificent bookstore must have taken over every thought in our minds. But, as I stared with my siblings at the tiny glass pebbles in the bookmark, it was perfectly clear.

They were the same multi-colored stones that resided in the simple-looking jar that currently rested on top of Mandy's desk. Our treasure-trove pebbles.

And that meant that, unexpectedly, the *stones* inside the memory jar, the very ones from this bookstore, were the last trinket on the list, the fifteenth one. RR...the Reading Retreat. The missing trinket *had* been in the jar after all.

I was suddenly beyond grateful that we had discovered the trinket list, leading us to the most special place in the world. Looking around at the enchanted book haven, I could also understand exactly why our parents had considered the stones as meaningful as the other trinkets. I knew that they would have been glad we visited it together, as a family.

As I thought about family, I looked over at our grandparents, sitting quietly together by the café. They looked back and waved. I smiled.

My brothers and sisters went off to get books of their own, wanting souvenir bookmarks to keep as well. I wandered toward the entrance of the building and strolled outside. This time, the colorful stones lining the pathway held my attention almost entirely.

I stopped by the beautiful, white fountain and admired its graceful form. I could picture my father walking by it too, and felt content. I looked over, into the water, and saw more of the colorful stones scattered across the bottom.

Pausing for a moment, I carefully pried off one of the stones from my bookmark and threw it into the fountain. It landed with a small bounce, making a soft 'plunk,' and then settled down amongst the others, where it would stay.

I was about to turn back, to go inside, when I noticed something strange on the ground, by the fountain's base. I crouched onto my knees and bent down. Then I let out a small gasp and ran my fingers over the hard cement, before getting up and returning to my family.

Carved in the sidewalk, written in the once-soft cement, and surrounded by small, multi-colored stones, were the initials of Will Avery's children. His own treasure-trove.

LaVergne, TN USA
28 July 2010
191194LV00006B/5/P